BROKEN

M. O'Keefe

PROLOGUE

THE BLOOD IN the air left a taste in the back of my mouth. Copper and familiar, like. Comforting almost. The taste of my childhood. Of Christmas and Saturday nights. Birthdays.

Poppy ran across the lawn, a ghost in the dark.

Go, I thought. *Go, princess.* My unspoken words were a hand at her back, pushing her faster. Further. She wouldn't go to the Constantines. I was sure of that. She'd been rattled by Caroline's manipulations.

I'd left my car down the road. The keys were in it. A stash of money. I had a man watching it; he would do what he could to get her into the car. Or follow her until she collapsed, and then he'd get her into the car.

Prayer had not been completely beaten out of me by the priests, and I sent whatever remained from deep in my gut heavenward. *Please get in that car.* Even if just to climb in the back seat and hide. Sleep off whatever Theo had drugged her with.

Up until ten minutes ago she'd been managing in the dark forest all on her own, sticking to the path like a good little girl. Theo had just been her driver. Caroline Constantine had been her kindly godmother and I'd been the wolf, taking bites out of her tender skin whenever I got the chance. But now everything was different. There was no path. Her house had been burned down. Caroline had been lying to her all along. Her driver was a spy for the Morelli's.

She needed to get the fuck out of this forest.

But she wasn't going to take help from the big bad wolf, I'd made sure of that.

She'd get to her sister. Poppy was smart. Capable. So fuckin' brave. She'd get to her sister and they'd take care of each other. I'd get word to Zilla, tell her they had to vanish and Zilla would get it done.

Goodbye, princess. Godspeed.

But then, in the dark of the yard, Poppy stopped.

No. No, baby. Don't do it.

But of course she did. She turned. Looked back at her house.

At me, standing here in the bright doorway. Well, that wasn't totally true. She turned back to look at the man she thought I was. The man she wished I was. I'd played so hard on that, using it to bend her. Manipulate her. Get between her legs.

She didn't know me. If she did, there'd be no looking back. Only a deep gratitude for escape.

It would be nice, though. To be the man she thought I was, even though that man was a son-of-a-bitch. A son-of-a-bitch, but not a monster, and the difference was a taste of something sweet after all these years of blood and rot.

Not for you, lad. Never was. Never can be.

The monster I truly was lifted the gun in my hand and pointed it at her. The stakes were high, and she needed to get away. From me. From all this shite. On the floor between my legs was Theo Rivers, the Morelli hit man I didn't see coming, breathing his last. "They . . . want . . . her," he gasped.

"They won't ever have her," I said. "Shut up and die, Rivers, you fuckin' cunt. There's nothin' for you here."

My eyes were still on Poppy. I imagined her in the dark. Her wide whiskey eyes. Her mouth.

Rivers laughed, the sound so absurd I looked down and found him lying in a growing pool of his own blood, more bubbling from his lips.

But he had another gun in his hand.

Pulled from a holster I hadn't seen from under his arm, he was pointing it at Poppy. My brain was a step behind, focused on Poppy, on what could never be mine. It was my only excuse, the only reason I'd fucked this up so bad.

"Dead or alive," he said and pulled the trigger. Rivers was former military, a sniper with an alarming number of kills. And even dying, he made the shot. In the dark of the yard, Poppy screamed and fell.

My brain blanked. I put a bullet in Theo's and ran to Poppy, sliding through the wet grass to fall at her side. The bullet from Theo's gun took a chunk out of her arm, a rough raw wound oozing fresh blood onto the grass. She was out cold from whatever shite Theo put in her.

Dead or Alive.

That was how the Morelli family wanted her. And the Constantines weren't going to be much better.

I fixed things. It was my value. It was why I was alive.

But I didn't know how to fix this.

CHAPTER ONE
Ronan

PITCH-BLACK, THE NIGHT howled. The wind rattled the shutters and swept over the chimney, creating a low moan that sounded like a wounded animal. In the hearth, the fire sputtered and then roared, sputtered and then roared again.

Dead or alive. Dead or alive.

"Didja hear me, boyo?" Sinead said, and I got out of the chair where I'd been slumped. Where I'd been getting too comfortable.

The whole cottage was entirely too comfortable. Unchanged, really, since my time as a kid. Small and low-ceilinged, full of books and soft chairs with blankets over the back. It smelled perpetually of tea and something baking.

The Dead or Alive orders changed everything. I couldn't just ship her off to Zilla with a target on her back. And I couldn't leave her alone. There was a good chance this was a mistake, but all I had left was a choice of mistakes. I had apartments and hidey-holes all over the world, full of money and guns and fake passports, but Caroline knew about too many of them. And I didn't trust Caroline. Not with Poppy.

Not anymore.

So, I'd made my way through an endless night. Back in time. To the one truly safe place I'd ever known.

Which happened to be right next to the most dangerous place I'd ever known.

That was a metaphor for something. Or a joke? I was just too tired to figure it out.

The only thing that mattered is that no one would find this place. No one would trace us across an ocean and through time zones back here. It had been a reckless and dangerous twenty-four hours. I'd called in every favor I had saved up over the years and burned through all my liquid cash, bribing everyone who needed it—and some who probably didn't—and got us here.

Now what?

"Ronan?"

"I heard you, Sinead," I said and walked across the wood floor to the stones of the kitchen off the back of the cottage. This part of the cottage was hundreds of years old. Part of a dairy for the church on the hill. "Do you have any coffee?"

"Tea," she said, coming up beside me. "I'll pick up some coffee tomorrow. But stop changin' the subject. What are you doin' with that lass?"

I had no fucking idea; that was the honest answer.

I needed more time. A few more days. A lot more information. But even if Poppy had answers, did she know them? More importantly, would she tell me?

Of course fucking not.

She had to believe I shot her, and I wasn't sure if telling her the truth was wise. Or merciful. I could handle her hate. I did not like it when she was scared. It made me want to be something I wasn't and could never be. Comforting.

Kind.

"She's scared." Sinead said it as an indictment of me, and that was more than fair. Sinead didn't know what was happening, but assuming it was my fault was always a safe bet.

"How do you know?"

"She told me!"

"She woke up?"

"For a few minutes about an hour ago. Asked what was happenin'."

"What did you tell her?"

"Nothin' because I don't fuckin' know what's happenin', do I?"

"I'll handle it."

She made that noise in the back of her throat that was pure Sinead. "You always were a cute hoor."

I smiled at the insult.

The night outside the window over the sink was black—no stars, no moon—except for the rectangles of light in the distance from the Catholic church that used to be a school. Someone was still there. In the vestry, if my memory was right. The rest of the building was dark, a looming shadow, blacker than the night around it.

"Where are the kids?" I asked. In my day, the building would be lit up like a carnival before the priests came in with the rods. More kids than beds. More beds than rooms. More chaos than sense. More pain than anything else.

Coming back here was a dangerous choice. But Theo Rivers didn't leave me with any.

The Constantines and the Morellis didn't leave me with any.

The unconscious girl in the bedroom, with stitches in her arm, didn't leave me with any.

Oh, lad, came my father's scathing voice in

my head. *You fucked this up proper.*

"It's not a parochial school anymore," Sinead said. "We made sure of that, but you didn't stick around long enough to see it done."

"Who lives there?"

"Father Patrick. He was new when you were here. You might not remember—"

"I remember," I said, my hand against the sink. The name stirred up the sleeping dogs in my head. Tommy and the cats.

Don't give 'em nuthin'.

"Look at the head on you, you scut," Sinead said. She was dressed in her coat with her keys in her hand, but she came back into the kitchen. "That girl's gonna be fine. But I'd wager money you haven't slept. Or eaten. There's soup and turkey in the fridge. Bread in the—"

"I'm fine."

"You look shite." She stood in front of me—all five feet of her. Her red hair going gray, and her bright blue eyes were as able to see through a lie as they ever were. It had been eight years since my stay at the school. Twelve years since Sinead brought as much kindness as she could to a feral Protestant kid in a brutal Catholic parochial school. If I had known her earlier, maybe there would have been a chance for me.

Still, when I showed up on her doorstep five hours ago, in the absolute dead of night knocking until she came to the door in her nightclothes, she recognized me right away.

"Ronan Byrne," she'd said, like it hadn't been years. She'd even smiled at me with a fondness I hadn't felt from anyone since her. "What's the craic?"

I'd told her I was in trouble and she opened that door up wide. Didn't even flinch when I carried Poppy, out cold, from the back seat of the banjaxed Taurus I'd bought off a father of two at the airport.

Years ago, when I first met Caroline, I'd thought she and Sinead were cut from the same cloth. Tough birds with soft spots for boys with criminal bents. I'd let that delusion color everything.

But Caroline and Sinead were nothing alike. Caroline worked the angles, figuring out how to make this situation turn up best for her.

Sinead just wanted to feed me.

"You should at least change your clothes," she said, pointing at the stack of clothes she'd gotten for me. "There's clean kex in there as well. Not sure they fit, but it's worth a try." Some other man's jeans. A cream sweater. Thick socks.

Underwear, apparently.

The white undershirt I wore was covered in blood. Poppy's blood.

It was still on my hands.

The wind felt like fingernails across my soul. God, I had forgotten the wind. Every minute here felt too long.

"I'll be back tomorrow," she said.

I shook my head. The Morellis had put out the Dead or Alive orders on Poppy. It was a fair guess they'd like me dead too. Caroline wanted both of us alive, but she wouldn't give a shit who got hurt in the process.

"Best stay away from us for a few days," I told her.

Sinead put her hand against my shoulder. I twitched, calming the urge to smack her hand away before I did it. "What are you doin', Ronan?"

"The less you know, Sinead," I said with as much reassurance as possible. Which, judging from her face, was not all that reassuring.

"Are you goin' to hurt that lass?" Sinead asked.

Yes. As bad as I can. As much as it takes.

"No. I'm gettin' her free of a net she was caught in."

"And you?"

Was I the net? Holding the net? Maybe I was caught in it too. Feck. I was bashed.

"I'm fine, Sinead. I always am. You know that."

"It's all right if you're not. Some adult in your life should have said that to you before it was too late."

"It was too late when I was born," I told her. "But thank you."

She pressed her lips tight, and I imagined there were a thousand things she might say about the boy I'd been and the night she'd saved me.

"Go," I told her. "We'll be fine. I'm going to change, eat something, and then talk to Poppy. Thank you, again, for the use of your cottage."

"You paid me."

"You didn't have to accept." Though it had been the kind of money a pensioner would be foolish not to accept.

"God, boyo." She sighed. "Look at what's come of you?"

I saw myself as she might. Too thin. I was always too thin for her. Exhausted. Bloody. A dangerous man with a dangerous amount of money and a bag full of guns.

I was what this place made of me, despite her

efforts to soften the edges.

Sinead left. And it was just the cottage, the moaning wind, and the dark outside.

The closed door to the bedroom.

Poppy.

Dead or Alive.

CHAPTER TWO

Poppy

I HURT. OH. I hurt. A lot. My head. My shoulder . . . what did I do . . . ?

Suddenly panicked, I opened my eyes. The ceiling was unfamiliar. A lamp beside my bed threw strange shadows across dark wooden beams, white plaster. A spider web of cracks in the corner. I was under a mountain of blankets that all smelled of cedar and mothballs. There'd been a woman?

A woman with graying red hair and worry on her face she couldn't hide.

There'd been a fire.

Which came first?

"Poppy?"

Ronan. Like a memory, the taste of him on my tongue came back to me. Salty and sweet. He'd kissed me, but wouldn't have sex with me. Had I begged? *Of course, I'd begged.*

But there was something else. A fight?

More than anything, I remembered being scared. My heart pounding in my throat. *I'm still scared.*

I'm scared of Ronan.

"I know you're awake." Ronan's voice was all sharp edges.

Fear crackled through me like ice, clearing my head, pushing the pain in my shoulder to some distant place. There, yes, but also not there at all. Using my good arm, I pushed myself up to sit. My other arm was in a sling, bound to my chest. A mountain of white gauze wrapped around my shoulder. My fingers were all pins and needles.

Ronan stood in the doorway. He looked tired. Haggard. His hair flopped down over his eyes. The white tee shirt he wore under his coat had blooms of rust-colored blood across his chest.

Mine? Or his?

"What happened to us?" I asked, my voice a croak.

"You don't remember?"

I shook my head, making my brain throb in my skull. I winced and pressed my hand to my head.

"I have medicine for you." From his coat pocket, he pulled two amber bottles. "Something for the pain and an antibiotic. And the doctor said you should drink more water. That might help with the headache."

He left and came back into the room with a glass of water, crossing from the doorway to the side of the unfamiliar bed. Despite his blood-stained shirt and grim face—despite my injury, despite not remembering what happened—I wanted him to come into the bed. To wrap those arms around me and hold me. Comfort me.

Tell me all the lies he'd been telling me all along.

But that was a luxury I could no longer afford. I was in danger; my whole body knew it.

And the danger was him.

"What happened to my arm?"

"A bullet grazed you."

"Grazed? It feels like it hit me."

"You have fifty stitches." He shook out the pills and I held out my hand, imagining the touch of his fingers against my palm as he set the pills against my skin. That small scrap of warmth. Of contact. Wanting it. Craving it. But instead of touching me, he set the pills down on the dark wooden table beside the bed, cluttered with reading glasses and novels that weren't mine.

Right. See, Poppy? He's making it clear.

With trembling hands, I picked up the pills,

set them on my tongue, and grabbed the glass of water. The glass was really heavy, and I spilled icy water down my neck and chest like a child. But he didn't help. He stood there and watched me fumble.

"What do you remember?" he asked.

"The taste of your come," I snapped, surprising myself. I even looked him in the eye when I said it. *Go ahead*, I thought. *Pretend nothing happened. Pretend you never touched me. But I won't play that game.*

He glanced away, out the window where the thick dark night pressed against the glass. "What else?"

"The way you held my head when you fucked—"

"Poppy!" He snapped and Lord, wasn't that something? Wasn't that *something*? This man rattled. This man showing me something he didn't want me to see.

I was still terrified, but I smiled at him, feeling not at all myself, and I liked it. My head hurt, my mouth tasted of cotton, and my shoulder screamed with every breath.

But I wasn't going to be this man's victim anymore.

"I don't remember getting shot," I said. "Or

getting stitches."

"Probably for the best."

"What day is it?" I asked.

"It's night."

"What night is it?"

His eyes were dark in his head and his face was drawn. Whatever had happened, he hadn't slept. "It's been twenty-four hours."

I gaped at him. "A full day?"

"What do you remember?" He said it slowly, biting off the edge of each word.

"I remember the fire. Going back to my house. You were worried about things happening that you didn't know about."

"You remember being in the senator's office in your house?"

"Yeah." The gaps in my memory were closing. The events of the night were spooling together, and a trembling kind of alarm filled me. I shifted to the other side of the bed away from where he stood, putting some distance between us. If he noticed, he didn't show me. "I do."

I'd been looking through the files in the banker's box the lawyer had given me, but something made me keep my mouth shut about that. Maybe he knew, maybe he didn't, but I kept it to myself. "Theo came in and . . . did he drug me?"

"Yeah."

"You were there." Oh Fuck. He'd been standing in the hallway of my house with a gun in his hand. I put my legs over the edge of the bed and got to my feet. I wasn't steady, but I was standing. "You killed the senator. You . . . shot him. That's what Theo said."

My head was light, and my body was heavy, and I couldn't run. I knew that. I was wearing a man's black dress shirt and nothing else. One sleeve had been torn off to accommodate my arm. The other hung past my hand and the hem went past my knees. It was Ronan's. The black shirt he'd been wearing in that hallway.

"You won't get far," he said, reading my mind. "If you try to run."

"You shot the senator. Tell me the truth."

"I did."

"Why?"

"Because it was my job."

"What kind of job is that?"

"Poppy, that's not important."

"You don't get to decide that! You don't get to decide any of this anymore."

"It was business."

"Whose business?"

The answer boomed in his silence. If we

didn't say the name, it wasn't true. Couldn't be real. But I was done pretending my world wasn't wrong.

"Caroline," I said. He nodded.

I stumbled back against the wall, knocking a picture cockeyed.

"She's not at all who I thought she was, is she?"

"She is. She's just other things as well."

There was no part of my life I could trust. No part of my life that I knew. This was a betrayal too big to process. And thinking about Caroline opened a giant hole in my belly, sucking me into nothing.

"Stop," he said, like he could read my mind. "Caroline doesn't matter right now. Put her away."

My laugh was hysterical. "Put her away?"

"Don't think about her."

His cold dead eyes indicated he had a tremendous amount of practice doing this. Just putting pain and hurt and betrayal and people away.

"This is how you survive," he said, and everything looped back to that night in the garden outside the party. The night we met. When all of this started.

Feeling pain was a choice. Feeling betrayed—

choice. And if all that was true, then strength was choice too.

Injured and bloody, I was going to choose strength.

Taking a deep breath, I squared my shoulders as best I could with the sling, inspired by the stone-cold killer in front of me.

"What was Theo's job? Since it clearly wasn't to be my driver."

"He was working for the Morellis. A spy and a hit man."

"A hit man?" I laughed, but he didn't. "That is . . . ridiculous."

He shrugged. "This is the world you live in now."

"Is that supposed to comfort me?"

"Do you remember what Theo said to you?" he asked, offering no words on the matter of comfort.

The memory was like trying to look at something underwater, distorted with the distance all off. I couldn't be sure if the memory were close or far. Real or fake. Then I realized it didn't matter. His questions were shit. Ronan stood there in a shirt stained with blood and the most important questions were actually mine to ask.

"Somebody shot me."

"Is that what you remember?"

"I don't..." I remembered running. That was all. Running and hearing a gun shot... "Theo is dead?"

He nodded.

"You shot him."

"He was going to kidnap you, Poppy. Take you to the Morellis, and who knows what they would have done to you?"

"Exactly what you did to me, I imagine," I said, liking the tartness of my words.

"They would make sure you *didn't* like it."

I flinched, his words hitting a soft spot I didn't want to have.

"Who shot me?" I pushed at my memories, trying to put the watercolor edges of the night together. *Ronan in a doorway. Yellow light and his black coat sweeping out behind him.*

He'd been holding a gun. At me.

I lurched out of the bedroom into a small living room. There was a crackling fire in a hearth and two chairs in front of it. A table cluttered with a teapot and mugs. Newspapers. More reading glasses. Knitting. Behind the table was a stone kitchen with a wall of windows looking out at the night. In the distance, there was another building with three bright windows.

The unfamiliarity of it all stopped me in my tracks.

"Where are we?" I asked. It was a home, like one from a movie. The kind that was immediately comfortable. The kind I never expected to find myself in.

"Someplace safe."

I laughed and shot him a caustic look over my shoulder. "If I'm with you, I can't be that safe."

"You are safe as I can make you."

"Did you shoot me?" I asked again.

"Is that what you remember?"

"Ronan," I said on a heavy sigh. "This sexy mysterious answering-a-question-with-another-question thing you're trying to do isn't going to work."

"It worked on you before." The corner of his lip lifted so fast it was like a spasm. An involuntary smile that pierced me right through the chest in a way I definitely didn't want.

"All part of the job?" I asked him, pretending as hard as I could to be as casual as he was.

He shrugged.

I crossed the rag rug on the wooden floor to the heavy door. He was behind me. Following me. And that was his choice. My mouth was dry, and my arm hurt, but if this man weren't going to give me answers, I could figure something out on my own.

"What are you doing?"

"Figuring out where we are."

With my good arm I threw open the door. Nothing but wind and darkness met me. Not even a moon or stars. No lights from other houses. Water was nearby and I could hear crashing waves. The wind blew me back a step, but I leaned forward and stepped out anyway. The chill and the damp went right through my shirt. Through my skin. Down to my bones. I turned and saw Ronan behind me. Following but not touching. Following and not stopping.

"Where the fuck are we?" I yelled so he could hear me over the wind.

"If I tell you, will you come inside?"

"Maybe."

"Northern Ireland."

My mouth fell open and I blinked, looking out at the darkness as if it were a different darkness than what I knew in New York.

"Poppy." He sighed. "Your shoulder."

"How did we get out of New York?"

"A private jet."

"Caroline's?"

"No."

"Whose?"

"I called in a favor," he said, like that was any kind of answer.

"Does she know where we are?"

"No."

That was . . . interesting. I would spin that around in my head later. The cold didn't allow me to dwell or think.

"Who took care of my arm?"

"A doctor."

"On the jet?"

He nodded.

"Another favor?"

"No. I paid him. I paid him to sew up your arm and to keep his mouth shut."

"You shot me?"

"If that's what you remember."

Right. This asshole right here. This dangerous, infuriating, murdering asshole. He didn't shoot me and then bring me all the way here. To fucking Northern Ireland.

"You're lying to me, Ronan." Funny, the courage being shot will drill down deep into your terrified soul. "What's the point of shooting me and then bringing me here?"

He rubbed a hand over his face, and I knew I was right. I almost felt bad for him.

"Is this . . . part of your job?" I asked.

"No." He laughed wearily. "No."

"Tell me what's happening," I demanded.

"Come inside and I will," he said, almost like he was asking. It's not like I really had a choice, but he pretended I did. That was a kindness from him I never expected. He wasn't one for leaving me with my dignity.

I walked past him in the doorway, letting my shoulder touch his chest, and he sucked in a breath like it burned.

I realized, standing with the fire in front of me and the night at my back, that my life was about doorways. The ones I went through. The ones I kept shut.

"Poppy?" he asked, close enough I could feel his breath against my face. The heat of him against my hurt arm. I couldn't step in or back. Or away. I was stuck there in that doorway with him. One more question on my lips.

"Was fucking me part of your job too?"

"I never fucked you."

"You know what I mean," I said, wanting the truth, even though I knew it would hurt.

The wind howled.

"Yeah," he said. "You were part of my job."

"There," I said and smiled with all my teeth.

"That wasn't so hard, was it?"

"Poppy." He reached for me, but finally, I stepped away into the room. The fire was hot, and the room swam a little around me. I stumbled, my knee suddenly buckling, and he grabbed me by my elbow, keeping me on my feet.

"You need to go back to bed," he said quietly. I wondered, looking at him, what doorways he'd walked through in his life and what he'd left behind in the process. Everything, I imagined. Ronan just kept walking, taking nothing with him through life.

That's not important. You need to focus on what's important.

"You didn't shoot me." It wasn't a question, but I would say nothing else to him if he didn't answer me.

"No," he confessed. "I didn't shoot you. Theo Rivers made an impossible shot."

"If I wanted to leave, would you let me?"

"You're hurt."

"Am I free to leave?" I looked him right in the eye with all the bravery I hadn't felt around him before.

"No. Not until we know what's happening. Not until we have a plan."

"I'm a prisoner?"

"The Morellis want you dead or alive," he said. "I'm not sure why you'd want to leave."

"Why?" What in the world did I mean to them dead or alive? "There's got to be a mistake."

"The Morellis don't make mistakes."

"Everyone makes mistakes." I had no idea why I was arguing like this. "Can't we just talk to someone? Eden Morelli! I could talk to her—"

"You're not talking to any Morellis."

"It's all just . . . a little intense, isn't it?"

"Yes, Poppy. It's intense." He was laughing at me. Not on the outside. On the outside, he was the same Ronan, deep and unreadable. But inside, I could tell he was having a good chuckle at my expense.

I sighed, suddenly exhausted.

"Come on," he said, putting a hand under my left elbow like I was eight years old or an invalid.

I flinched away from him. "I don't need your help."

He humored me all the way back into the bedroom. "Of course not."

I had seven million more questions, but the adrenaline was gone, and I limply climbed into the bed that wasn't mine. My mind was fuzzy from the pain meds. I could ask all of them, but they were all extensions of the only question that mattered. The only question I had the strength to ask as my eyelids drooped and my body went heavy.

"Why?" I whispered. Why did Ronan shoot the senator? Why did Theo drug me? Why did the Morelli family want me dead or alive? Why did he save me?

He tucked blankets around me. If I had the strength, I would push him away. *Fuck you, Ronan*, I thought, my mind drifting toward sleep. *Fuck you.*

"I don't know why," he said. "That's what's killing me."

CHAPTER THREE

Poppy

IT WAS EARLY when I woke up. The sky curled up on its gray edges, revealing its pink belly. Out the window, I could see the tops of the hills, green and rolling, studded with rocks. I sat up, listening for what, I wasn't sure. Ronan in the other room. A conversation. A city or town outside the walls. A highway. But there was nothing but silence, silence like a thick blanket over this little house.

Northern Ireland.

I had no reason not to believe him, except, of course, I couldn't believe anything he said.

Carefully, I got to my feet. The smell of my body—blood and sweat—wafted from the warm white sheets. I needed a shower. Clean clothes.

But what I really needed was to get in touch with my sister.

The thought of her, of Zilla, made me stronger. Focused. I had to get the fuck out of here and find Zilla.

I slipped off the sling, wincing as my right shoulder burned at the motion. I unwrapped the gauze around my arm until I came to a wide bandage. Wincing, I peeled off the adhesive tape enough that I could lift the corner of the bandage and reveal a jagged wound, stitched up tight with dark even stitches. Fifty of them. I pressed the tape back down but left off the gauze.

There was a bench at the foot of the wooden bed; on it was a stack of clothes. I pulled on the sweatpants and drew the drawstring tight. There were thick white socks that were not easy to negotiate but I got them on too. Then I searched the room for a phone. Not just my cell phone, which felt like a total dream, but a landline. A laptop. A desktop. A homing pigeon. Anything.

But there were only books and reading glasses and under the bed . . . a cat.

"Where did you come from?" I whispered to the gigantic black and brown cat with whiskers that touched the floor. She meowed at me like I took her spot and she hated me for it. "Well," I told her. "You can have the bed back. I'm leaving."

There were two doors in the bedroom. The second door led to a white-tiled, windowless bathroom with an old-fashioned clawfoot tub with a shower along one wall. My body absolutely longed to sit in a warm bath, but there was no time. I peed quickly and avoided looking at myself in the mirror as I washed my hands.

The door leading to the main room was cracked open, revealing the two chairs in front of the fireplace. The door squealed as I pushed it open enough so I could slip out. The cat followed me. The fire had died, and the room was cold and sharp.

Winter cold in June.

Ronan sat in one of the chairs in front of the empty fireplace. Sleeping. He still wore his jacket, the bloodstained undershirt. Like he'd tucked me in last night, came out here, and just collapsed.

At rest, he looked so different. It made me realize how alive he was when awake. How the air and space around him thrummed and crackled. Asleep, he was smaller. Nearly . . . sweet. I could see in the corners of his mouth and the droop of his shoulders—the boy he'd been, wild and smart.

And very alone.

His hair was down over his face and I clenched my hand against the urge to sweep it back. I had to burn away this stupid tenderness I felt for him. This lingering curiosity. I had leaned toward him—against him—because I was weak. And scared. And childish.

I needed to be the opposite.

Everything between us had been an act. There was nothing for me with him.

Quiet, I snuck around the room and kitchen, looking for a phone. No luck. Not even a landline or a computer. Had Ronan cleared the house of all the ways I could communicate or were we just that remote?

I looked at the back of his head as I stood in the kitchen. He had a phone on him for sure. In the pocket of his coat, probably. If I were braver, I'd go through those pockets.

And if I was feeling braver these days, having my back against the wall would be a great reason for that, but I wasn't *that* brave.

He had a gun balanced on his knee. If I stepped over there and touched him, he'd be awake in a heartbeat. Probably would have me on the ground with the gun pressed to my head.

Yeah, we'll skip that.

The cat, however, had jumped up on the table beside his chair, almost knocking over a pair of reading glasses. She sniffed him, one paw reaching forward to test his arm.

"No," I whispered. "Kitty!" I made a kissing

noise the cat didn't care about. All I needed was this cat to wake him up and accidentally get killed.

In one of the cupboards, there'd been some kibble and cans of wet food. At the sound of me opening one of those cans as quietly as I could, the cat forgot her interest in Ronan and came to curl around my legs as I emptied the food into the bowl.

There, kitty, try not to wake up the killer in the chair. I know he smells good.

The cat fed, I left the kitchen and stepped wide around Ronan to the front door. Plugging my feet into an old pair of muddy, green, rubber boots, I opened the front door as quiet as a mouse. Looking for a way out, I slipped into the cold unknown.

The cottage was small and white walled with dark beams and a roof made from thatch. Actual thatch. If I hadn't been kidnapped and held against my will by a man I—against all better judgment—still wanted to fuck, I might marvel at such a thing. But I was a little bit busy.

A big tall church made of red brick with a thin spire sat on top of the rocky outcrop behind the cottage about a hundred yards away. Around the two buildings was nothing but wilderness. No trees. Only grass and rocks. Low scrub. Stone fences. A landscape alive and green and real and still somehow as desolate as the moon. The sky loomed and towered. There was so much of it and so little of me.

I turned in a circle. The dirt driveway ended at a gravel road that stretched into nothing in either direction. The rolling green hill to my left dropped off to what looked and sounded like an ocean. Past the hill was nothing but black water.

To the right were . . . sheep?

My chest cracked wide, pried open by the howling wind and the salt air. I was terrified in a way. And something else. Something I hadn't ever felt before. Something I didn't know how to name. But I felt very alive in this moment. Almost painfully so. Tears burned my eyes.

There was a car in the driveway I didn't recognize, but I quickly opened the driver's-side door. It smelled of cigarette smoke, and there were no keys. Not in the middle console or under the mat or tucked in the visor or any of the other places where people in the movies hid keys in cars.

Theo the spy/hit man never got around to teaching me how to hot-wire a car and so, quiet as I could, I shut the car door.

A dead end.

Which left me with the gravel road. Or the church behind the cottage.

I followed the dirt trail around the house and across the green field, up the stone steps set into the rocky outcropping. This was a well-worn path, the stones smooth in the middle. I imagined a hundred years of feet making use of these stairs and liked the thought.

The fresh air crackled in my lungs and woke me up, but I was easily winded. I stopped, leaning against one of the stone fences to catch my breath, wondering if maybe I'd bitten off more than I could chew for one day. I didn't even have a coat.

But getting to Zilla was the goal.

God, I should have a plan for this first. Like, was I going up to that church and telling people I was kidnapped? By a killer who'd saved me from another killer? The cops would get called. Or worse. If I asked to use a phone, there would only be more questions.

Perhaps I should just head back, get my bearings. But Ronan had made a mess of my bearings. I couldn't trust him, and I couldn't trust myself around him.

A man came out one of the side doors of the church. He lifted an arm in my direction and I lifted my good arm back at him.

It was funny what Ronan did to me.

I'd been a naive fool all this time, pushing the truth away when it was staring me right in the face. Keeping my head in the sand and believing the best about people when they'd given me no evidence of their best.

Ronan came along and changed that.

Suspicion and bravery were not traits that came naturally to me, but I got to my feet anyway, suspicious of a man coming out of a church, and bravely went to meet him. And that was new.

Maybe I was new.

God, please let me be new.

"Are you all right, lass?" The man asked once he got close enough down the stone steps. He wore a priest's collar and black shirt with a brown cardigan thrown over it. He was on the young side of middle age and tall. Broad and upright through the shoulders. Close-cropped brown hair. All around a handsome man.

"Fine," I said. "Just taking in the view."

He smiled at me like I was a Christmas morning. "Where did you come from? I don't see a lot of new faces around here."

"The cottage," I said, pointing back at the tiny little building nestled in the folds of the hills.

There was no smoke from the chimney, so I guessed Ronan was still sleeping. But for how long? He'd come find me and then what? Adrenaline made sweat break out along my hairline. The clock was ticking.

"Sinead's gaff?" he asked. The wind blew his brown hair over his face and he swept it back. "Where's Sinead?"

"We rented it for a few days."

"We?"

"My . . . husband and I."

Oh, wow. The lies just fell off my lips. There was no reality in the universe where Ronan and I ended up married.

"I didn't know Sinead did that," he said. "Sorry, my manners." He tugged on his sweater, swept a hand down the front of his shirt. "I'm Father Patrick."

"I'm Poppy . . . Smith." Lord, I could practically see my sister rolling her eyes at me.

"Nice to meet you, Poppy. You don't look too sure-footed. Can I walk you back to the cottage?"

"Actually," I said. "I'd like to go see the church if you don't mind."

Delight widened his eyes. "Grand. Of course. Let me . . ." He held out his elbow and I took it gratefully up the last of the stairs. At the top, I dropped his arm and stepped to the side, putting more distance between us. "You and your husband, you're traveling, like?"

It was nice hearing Ronan's accent and turns of phrase in this man's voice. Made me miss that man at the party in the dark. The man who never was. "Yeah. Yes. It's our honeymoon."

"Oh, you shouldn't be wasting time with the likes of me and this old church," he said, blushing and looking at me out of the corner of his eyes.

"My husband is sleeping." *Forgive me, God and Father Patrick, for the lie.*

The wind practically blowing us sideways, we walked by a fenced garden the size of the cottage down the hill and a small shed with a cow chewing grass outside of it.

"You're a farm too?" I asked, voice raised to be heard over the wind.

"Well, the village is far away when I run out of cream," he yelled back. "Come. Let's get a cup of tea in you before you catch a chill."

"You might be too late," I said through chattering teeth.

The door built into the side of the church was a heavy thing made to withstand Viking raiders and English soldiers. Father Patrick probably got those shoulders of his from opening this door day in and day out. He wrenched it open with his whole body and stood aside as I entered a small stone alcove. Two steps led up to a dark hallway that opened into the sanctuary and two small steps led down to a dark hallway that opened into a wood-paneled room.

The door slammed shut behind us and the silence was suddenly very loud. I had the extremely disconcerting thought that I wasn't sure I could open that door on my own if I had to.

"Follow me," he said.

We took the two stone steps down to the wood-paneled room.

"This is the vestry," he said, rushing ahead of me to move books off a chair and a sweater that he threw in the corner. It was like visiting a boy in his college dorm, except the boy was a priest and a fire crackled in the fireplace. "Looks a bit shabby, I reckon, but when it's just me, there's not much reason for housekeeping."

"It's fine," I said. "Cozy." The wood paneling was carved with acorns and vines. The top half of the windows was diamond-shaped stained glass.

"Grand, won't you sit down?" He stepped over to a low hutch where there was an electric tea kettle and a tin of cookies. He shut a door that had been open, revealing what looked like a bedroom.

"It's a church and a small farm and you live here too?" I asked.

"Aye. St. Brigid's used to be a school too," he said, smiling at me over his shoulder.

"A school?" A tingle started in the back of my brain.

"Of a kind," he said. "Parochial. A sort of juvenile detention for court-placed kids."

Juvie, I thought. In a church?

The priests liked my surrender. That was something Ronan had said to me. The priests here? Why would he bring me back here?

"How long have you been here?" I asked.

"Oh. Ages," he said. "Twelve years." The whistle on the kettle blew and a minute later, he came over with cups of tea and a chagrined smile to where I was sitting. "I added sugar and milk. I'm not used to people visiting, so I just made it the way I like it before I thought to ask."

"It's fine. Thank you."

Father Patrick sat in the chair across from mine with a happy groan. "Are you from the States?" he asked, and I nodded. "This is a pretty lonely place for a honeymoon."

"My husband is from here."

"County Antrim?"

"Is that . . . is that where we are?"

His eyebrows furrowed, and I'd revealed too much. "He's from a tiny town. A sheep pasture, he said."

"Well, there's plenty of those around here."

"Are you here by yourself?"

Father Patrick nodded. "During the week. Sunday mass, I have a few visitors. Not as many as I used to but . . ." He gave me a bright smile. "St. Brigid's flock is small but mighty."

I took a sip of the tea, which was exactly what I needed—warm and sweet.

"How about you?" he asked. "What do you do at home?"

A bitter laugh slipped out of me. I'd been put in charge of a foundation that probably wasn't even real. I was the widow of a man I hated. The pawn of a powerful woman. "Nothing," I said with every bit of honesty I had in me. "I am nothing back home."

"No one is nothing," he said quietly.

I'd been a sister, perhaps my only success, and Zilla might consider that marginal.

"I wanted to be a teacher," I said, for absolutely no good reason, except this man made me long to be a version of myself I could be proud of.

"Brilliant," he said. "What grade?"

"Fifth."

"Ah. Not quite teenagers but no longer kids. A good age."

"You were a teacher too?"

"Wanted to be, like you." He shrugged, his eyes on his tea.

"And then you found the church?"

"No. Actually, I was hoping to be a teacher within the church. But the Lord had other plans." A wave of melancholy rolled over the room. "Ach," he said with a grin. "Would you like to come see the sanctuary? It's a modest church but it was built in the 1700s and the altar was carved out of the jaw of a whale that had washed up on the beach in Carrickfergus."

"You're joking."

"I would not joke about our holy altar. Or our eight bells cast by Rudhall." He stood. "Come on, then." He led the way up the two steps and down the other hallway that opened into the sanctuary. It was dark and quiet. The beautiful light wood pews were empty but glowing. The ceiling soared over our heads.

"It was built on a Celt holy site by monks who'd fought off the Vikings and the Normans. It was burned down. Twice." He grinned at me and the affection he had for this building was sweet.

Moving, really. "The IRA used to meet here too. The front door still has bullet holes from a fight with the English soldiers during The Troubles."

The morning sun was coming in through the east windows, lighting up the stained glass. Christ in yellow and red wearing a thorn crown and a purple robe was partially obscured by a chain link over the glass.

"Why is the fencing on the inside?" I asked.

"A remnant from when the church was a parochial school." His smile was rueful. "The students threw rocks from the pews."

"You haven't taken it down?"

"There's no money. Or help." He shrugged. "It's also a good reminder."

"Of what this place was?"

"Of what it never should have been."

His words were so fierce, there was nothing to say in the face of them. The church didn't mean much to me, but it was beautiful and quiet. Holiness came from work; I understood that. It came from suffering and trial. It was the quiet after the storm, the rest after the battle, and this building had seen its share of battles. Its holiness was hard won.

It reminded me just a little of Ronan sleeping in the chair. His rest well earned.

Blasphemous, I know.

I wished I could pluck these thoughts out of my head, this softness out of my heart, because he didn't deserve any of it. But I didn't know how. Wanting what I shouldn't was sort of my thing. My stupid, gullible thing.

"Come," he said. "Let me show you the whale bone." He stepped past the pulpit just as thunder split the sanctuary's quiet. The doors at the end of the center aisle rattled loud and hard.

"What in the name of the Father?" Father Patrick asked, stepping back and away from the doors like they might blow in.

But I knew. The devil had come, and my time was up.

"Do you have a cell phone?" I asked.

"A what?" Father Patrick, who had been living alone and in silence with a cow, was not keeping up with the sudden change of pace I'd brought to his life. Hell was coming through his doors, and I was running out of time.

CHAPTER FOUR

POPPY

"A PHONE, FATHER Patrick. Do you have a phone?"

"Sure," he said, blinking at me.

"Can I have it?"

"What?" Even as he didn't understand, he was fishing it out of his pants pocket. The door rattled again, and whatever invaders those doors had kept out in the past were nothing compared to Ronan.

Father Patrick's phone was several years old and didn't have a passcode on it. It also didn't have any bars.

"There's no service," he said. "You have to go into the village. What . . . what is going on? Are you safe? Are we . . . safe?"

"You're fine. I'm fine. I just need to get a message to my sister, and I lost my phone."

"Your husband doesn't have one?"

"Lost his too. They were stolen. In the airport." These were dumb lies.

"There's a landline in the vestry—"

There was sudden silence outside, and I knew Ronan was walking around the building looking for another door.

"I don't have time for that."

"You're not on your honeymoon, are you?" Father Patrick asked.

"I am," I said as I plugged my sister's phone number into the father's phone. "I totally am. Next time you're in town, could you just text that number and tell her Poppy is . . . is . . . wherever we are?" I handed the phone back to the wide-eyed Father Patrick. "I swear," I said, not letting go of the phone he was holding. "Everything is fine. I just need to get a message to my sister. Tell her I'm safe."

The big doors on the side of the building were wrenched open, letting in a gust of wind that pushed me forward.

"Poppy!" Ronan's voice thundered with the pound of his feet up the stairs. "Where—?"

"Here, darling!" I said with a wide smile, turning to an enraged Ronan as he came into the sanctuary. Oh, he looked wild. Blood-stained and ready for battle. The fiercest thing I'd ever seen in my life. Something low and thrilling sizzled through me and I tried very hard to pretend it didn't.

"Hello!" I rushed toward him, trying to hide the gun in his hand from the priest's eyes. "Put it away," I whisper-yelled at him and then curled my arm through his, facing the priest again with a smile. Ronan slipped the gun down the back of his pants. "I just went for a walk," I said. "While you slept. How are you feeling?" I cooed. If he had any reaction to my touch or my coos, he didn't let on. Instead, he stared at Father Patrick.

The rattled priest attempted to stare back but couldn't manage the cold menace Ronan was projecting all over the place.

"Darling," I said, squeezing Ronan's arm. "Let me introduce Father Patrick. Father Patrick, this is my husband Ronan . . . Smith."

"Good to meet you," Father Patrick said with a trembling nod. Ronan, of course, said nothing. Under my hand, his arm was hard. Every muscle flexed.

"We should go," I said with a smile that made no sense considering the tension in the room. Pretending really was my one great skill. "It was lovely to meet you, Father. And thank you for the tea and the tour."

"My pleasure," he said with a sincere if fleeting smile. "Come back any time."

I turned, tugging Ronan with me, but he stood like a post. Unmoving. Staring at the priest.

"Do you remember me?" Ronan asked, his voice set so low, the hair on the back of my neck stood.

"Should I?" Father Patrick asked with raised eyebrows. "Are you from the village?"

"No." Ronan said nothing else. Made no other move. Just stood there. An apex predator staring down something he wanted to tear apart.

"Ronan," I whispered. "My shoulder hurts."

I had sincere doubts there was anything I could do that would move him to action, but I was wrong. He sucked in a deep breath and turned, his arm around my waist.

"Are you all right?" he asked.

"Just sore."

He nodded and turned us around toward the door, still open.

"Goodbye," I said cheerily over our shoulders, pretending nothing strange at all had happened.

Soon, we were out on the rocky green hilltop. The sun was up over the water, covering us in buttery yellow sunlight.

Without looking at me, Ronan stepped free of my touch and the wind moaned around us. Between us. Its cold fingers reached into the collar of my shirt. The tops of my boots.

"You can't do that, Poppy," he said, his eyes on the horizon.

"Talk to priests?" I tried to make a joke, but judging by his face, he wasn't going to find me funny. Not ever again.

"Leave without telling me."

"I forgot," I said. "I'm a prisoner."

"Not a very good one."

"Well." I grinned at him. "I would argue a prisoner is only as good as her prison."

"Jokes, now? Do you forget there's a family of killers who want you dead or alive?" He looked over my shoulder. "He's watching."

Ronan walked away and down the stone steps, his black coat flaring behind him like dark wings. He expected me to follow and that was certainly my plan, but I'd been shot and drugged and hadn't eaten anything in a few days, and probably shouldn't be out climbing across Irish cliffs.

Light-headed, I sat on the stone fence that seemed to be here for exactly this purpose. Another cat jumped on a rock further up the hill, different from the one in the cottage. This one was all black and slinky and small. She was coming to investigate me.

"Poppy?" I heard Ronan call from a distance

and I waved at him to keep going. I just needed a second. And a sandwich.

"I'm fine," I said. "Just a little—"

Like we were in a Brontë novel, Ronan swept me up in his arms and curled me close to his chest. "You don't have to—"

"Shut up, Poppy," he said, the muscles in his jaw all tense. The tendon in his neck stood out against his pale skin and I could smell him. He was warm and real. His arms were around me. His breath was in my hair. The beat of his heart was right there in the tender skin of his throat. The cold of the wind was gone and left just heat in his arms.

"Were you scared?" I asked. "For me?"

His silence wouldn't be broken, so I took one more look at the blue of his eyes. How, from this angle, they glowed like the sky above us. Then I put my head down on his shoulder, reminding myself this was nothing to him.

I was nothing.

He kicked open the door to the cottage and ducked inside the low doorway. I slowly put my feet on the ground. His arm against my back stayed there until he knew I was steady.

"All right?"

"Yes. Thank—"

"What the fuck did you tell him?" He grabbed my arms hard enough that I winced and tried to step away, but he pulled me up on his toes.

"Nothing."

"Poppy!" He yelled loud enough my hair blew back and I saw in his eyes how scared he was. For me. Oh, how easy it would be to melt into this. Into his concern and ferocious worry. How easy it would be to believe it meant something when it was only instinct for him. Possession and control.

"I told him we were married. On our honeymoon."

His face relaxed. "What else?"

I kept my mouth shut about my sister. "Nothing. We talked about the church. How it used to be a school."

"You're lying to me, Poppy."

"Well, Ronan, you're lying to me." I sounded good and strong. Righteous. But my head was swimming.

"Sit down before you fall down."

Gladly. I collapsed carefully into one of the comfortable chairs in front of the fireplace. Where there was no fire.

"Do you know how to make a fire?" I asked, cold all the way through. "I'd do it, but I don't know how."

Of course he knew how to build a fire.

Silent, he set small kindling and a lit match. He added larger pieces of wood, crouched, and blew on the embers, and it was so sexy and intimate I had to look away. The wood popped and Ronan got back on his feet.

"Where's your sling?" He asked.

"I took it off."

"The bandages?"

"I left one on. I'm a terrible prisoner and patient. What can I say?"

"How is your arm?"

"It hurts."

He looked at me like *That is what you get*, and I couldn't argue.

In front of me was a tufted ottoman and he sat on it, grabbing the big heavy chair I sat in by the arms and pulling it close until my knees hit the insides of his thighs. I tried to pull back, but there was nowhere to go.

"What did you really tell him?"

"That we were married and on our honeymoon," I repeated.

"You're not as good at lying as you think, Poppy. Did you use a phone? Call your sister?"

I bit my lip, wondering what was smart. Trusting him seemed stupid. He looked up and blew out a long slow breath. God, he looked tired. "I can't keep you safe if you don't tell me what happened."

"I'm trying to keep my sister safe," I whispered.

He reached forward and touched my cheek. I was crying. "I know," he said. "Me too. And if she knows where we are, she's not safe."

I sucked in a breath. The thought hadn't occurred to me. "I gave the priest her phone number and asked him to call her the next time he was in town. Tell her where we are."

"Damnit, Poppy," he said, dropping his head so it very nearly rested on my chest. How amazing would it be if he were to lean against *me?* Just take a second to catch his breath and get his bearings?

But Ronan didn't lean against anyone. Not for any reason. And the few inches between us might as well have been miles.

"I'll just go back up there and tell Father Patrick to forget it. I'll erase her number," I offered.

"You're not going anywhere near that place. I'll handle it."

He shoved the chair back and I winced as my shoulder hit the top of the armrest. Not that he noticed.

He was too big for the small cheerful cottage. Too menacing in the bright kitchen where he couldn't look more out of place if he tried. He pulled out a pot from the fridge and a loaf of bread wrapped in a linen towel from a drawer.

"How will you handle it?" I asked him.

"You think I'm going to kill a priest?" he asked, like it was a joke.

"I'm asking because I don't know what you'll do. I don't know you at all."

He struck a match and lit the stove. Set the pot on the burner and then found a long serrated knife and cut thick slices off the bread.

I stood, walking into the kitchen. "Father Patrick said the church used to be a school—"

"Sit down," he said, but I ignored him.

"Was this the school you went to? When you were a kid? The priests who hurt you?"

"I'm not talking about this with you."

"Did Father Patrick—?"

"Sit the fuck down, Poppy."

"Why would you bring me here if—?"

It was like he flew across the kitchen, grabbing my elbows and pulling me up against his body. His eyes were wild on mine. "Do you think I want to be here? Do you think I would be here if there was any other choice?"

He wrapped one arm around my waist and for a second, I thought he was going to kiss me, and I was breathless wanting it. Hungry for it. But he lifted me off my feet and walked me to the bedroom. Once inside, he put me on my feet and stepped away so fast I wobbled.

"Ronan? What—?"

He left without a word, and the sound of the door being locked from the outside was so loud I flinched. "Ronan?" I walked over to the door and tried to open it, but he really had locked it. "Ronan! What the hell are you doing?"

Silence was my only answer. I screamed and pounded until I was weak. Until I was empty. Until I was remembered who he was. And who I was to him.

Nothing.

And the galling thing, the truly galling thing, was I'd been here before. I'd been here so many times in my life, and every time before I'd just curled up and let someone else's opinion of me be the only thing that mattered.

Well. Fuck. That.

I was different. If I was going to survive this and save my sister, I had to be.

Ronan didn't know who he was dealing with. I didn't, either, really. But I was ready to find out.

CHAPTER FIVE
RONAN

PIKEY TOM WAS a kid who'd slept in the bunk across the hallway from mine at St. Brigid's. I had no idea if he was really a Traveller, but he introduced himself to everyone as Pikey Tom, and if you said anything about it, he'd punch you in the throat. That he let me call him Tommy had seemed like a badge of honor. That we became friends was even more so.

He was the same age as me, and by the time I'd showed up in that hallway, he'd already been there awhile. And he was an absolute legend. He'd thrown rocks at the stained glass from inside the sanctuary, rumor had it he'd bitten the earlobe off one of the priests, and he'd tried to escape three times. At bedtime, Father McConal himself came and locked him to his bed with handcuffs.

"Ah, you like this, don't you, you dirty fecking pervert," he'd spit at the old man.

For whatever reason, Tommy had liked me.

Or maybe he'd just pitied me—scrawny and far more scared than I was going to admit. And that had been enough for friendship at St. Brigid's. That first night, he'd taught me the most important lesson surviving that place.

We owe 'em nothing and we give 'em nothing.

"Them," of course, being the priests.

He told me not to cry or apologize. To never—no matter what they did to me—ask for forgiveness.

That's how they get you.

It had been hard, that first month, not crying. But by the second month, I was stone dry. The priests wanted us to apologize for who we were and how we'd been raised and the things we couldn't control and the ways we'd never been taught any better. But all those things were how we'd survived. And those boys who'd cracked under the prayers and the beatings and the fasting and the work, and begged for atonement for the sins they didn't even understand, walked around with their eyes glowing with zeal and hot food.

Fuck them cunts, Pikey Tom had always said.

"Fuck them cunts," I said now, staring up at the church until the kettle whistled.

I doubted Poppy was awake. The daft girl had been practically asleep on her feet, but she needed food, so here I was, putting a tray of lunch together for her.

I also needed answers and her back under my control. I needed her to think we were a team until I figured out what the Morellis wanted, and only then could the mistakes I'd made regarding one Poppy Maywell be forgotten.

Don't cry. Don't apologize. Don't ask for forgiveness.

As a motto, it had served me just fine. I wasn't going to change it now.

I unlocked the bedroom door and knocked before pushing it open. Pretending at manners. The room, without the heat from the fire, was cold.

You didn't think of that, did you, you edjit? my father taunted in my head.

"Poppy?" I called. The window up near the ceiling was too small for her to climb through.

"In the bathroom."

"You decent?" I asked, standing in front of the shut bathroom door.

"Does it matter?" Ah, my princess still had some claws.

"Well, if you're taking a shit—"

"Jesus Christ, Ronan. I'm in the bath."

I opened the door, expecting to see her hiding

beneath the water with only her head visible. But whatever motto Poppy had been living with to keep herself safe before she'd been shot, kidnapped, and taken to Ireland was gone.

My princess was turning into a queen.

She sat in a bath so hot steam rose off the water, curling around her hair that hung down her back and over her collarbones in damp blond curls. She was leaning against the porcelain, a towel between her skin and the cold tub. The water lapped at the underside of her breasts. Pink from the heat. Nipples hard in the cooler air. Her skin was flushed and creamy and I, like I always did around her, felt my dick go hard from one heartbeat to the next.

Poppy was thinner than she should be, but her tits were perfection. The things I wanted to do to them . . .

"This bother you, Ronan?" she asked. With her good arm, she lifted the washcloth and squeezed water over her neck and chest. Water trickled over her nipples.

Jesus Christ. This fucking girl. All I needed right now was Poppy being brave. Bold. I needed meek Poppy. Scared and submissive Poppy. Not this . . . goddess.

"No," I lied. "You aren't supposed to be getting the stitches wet."

"I'm not."

She'd taken off the tape and the bandage. Tight, black surgical stitches started in the front of her armpit and went all the way around to the back. The skin was puffy and pink but not red. "The doctor said you needed to keep it dry."

"I am."

"Have you taken the medication—?"

"You locked me in the goddamned room, Ronan. You can stop pretending you care."

"Did you take the meds?" I asked again because I cared. I cared too fucking much.

"Yes, Daddy."

Oh, that fucking girl. She wanted to play Daddy games? I could—

I jerked away from that thought. "I thought you'd be hungry."

"Starving," she said, clearly attempting an innuendo. I smiled, but she couldn't see it as I put the tray down on the sink. "You want to come in?" she asked, bending her legs so her knees poked out of the water. "You look like you could use a bath."

She wasn't wrong, but I shook my head at her.

"Suit yourself," she said with a shrug that

made her tits wobble. Light from the open door behind me licked her skin the way I wanted to.

"Have you seen the cat?" she asked.

"What cat?"

"The one that lives under the bed. There's another one out on the stone steps."

Tommy and those fucking feral cats.

"I haven't seen any cats."

Poppy watched me from the bath in a way that was suddenly disconcerting. Something had changed. Some small thing, and she was different.

Poppy had brown eyes, and when I'd met her in that side yard that night she'd been sold off to the senator, she'd looked like one of the deer that showed up on this hilltop all the time. Wide-eyed and wild. And young. Too young.

Now, her eyes glowed like the whiskey I could use right now, and they were narrowed like she would take me out if she could. Fuck, if I didn't like that.

She'd been a blonde the night I met her, and every time I saw her after that at a gala or a function, careful not to be seen by her, she had still been a blonde. But that day in her kitchen, when Caroline took me to have a word with the senator, the brilliant natural red of her hair had been coming in at the roots.

She'd dyed it blond again, but the red was coming back.

Like it was just inevitable.

"I need some answers," I said.

"Funny. Me too."

I rubbed a hand over my face, hiding my smile. Fuck. I was exhausted. But this Poppy... naked and angry... this Poppy was going to a problem. In more ways than one. We'd been in the wind for almost two days already and I didn't know how many more we had.

"I called your sister before we left the States," I told her, giving her the information most likely to win her to my side. "I used your phone and then destroyed both our phones."

"What did you tell her?" she asked, sitting up, and I made no effort to hide how I watched her body.

"I gave her an address in London. Told her she needed to get there as fast as she could and to tell no one where she was going. I let her know that you were safe and we'd be in touch."

"What did she say?"

"She threatened to castrate me if I hurt you."

She sat back with a sigh and smile. "Classic Zilla."

"She threatens castration a lot, does she?"

"Actually, yes." She bit her lip, pushing a small mountain of suds back and forth between her hands. I refused to follow the movement, even though I starved for the glimpses of her body revealed and then hidden. "Is she there? At that address?"

"I gave you an answer. Now I get one."

"You won't get shit from me unless I know my sister is safe."

"As safe as I could make her. Now you really owe me an answer."

"We've played this game before." She was so bold looking up at me through her lashes. But I still saw that fear. That was the balance between us: fear and arousal. I'd played on it before and I could do it again. Hold myself distant while pulling her close.

Not sure why it seemed so fucking hard right now, but it did.

I stood and shrugged out of my jacket. It fell in a heap on the floor and the cool air woke me up, straightened my spine.

"That game isn't fun anymore," she said, pursing her lips and tucking her hair back.

"Sure it is."

"It wasn't real," she said. "You were only pretending."

"You were a job, Poppy," I told her. Lied to her, really. Poppy was never part of the job and killing the senator hadn't been an order from Caroline. But the truth behind both of those things didn't serve anyone right now. It would make the shitstorm we were caught in worse.

"Right."

"But I wasn't pretending," Through my dark pants, I cupped my aching cock in my hands, and Poppy—my beautiful girl, my beautiful curious girl—couldn't help but watch. "I fucking want you, Poppy. From the second I met you, I've wanted you. That is very real."

She licked her lips and glanced away, trying to be strong, only to glance back. She was breathing hard. Her skin was pinker than before. Those fucking nipples . . .

"What do you want?" she whispered. Poppy liked filthy intentions spelled out with dirty words. I could give her that. Because it would give me something I wanted.

"To get my mouth on those tits," I told her. She put a hand against her breast. Her right shoulder still and dry.

"What else?" she whispered.

"Put my hand between your legs." She sucked in a breath and another one. "I want to make you come so hard, you break, Poppy. You break wide fucking open for me. I want you wet and I want you broken."

That was very much the truth.

"Why was I job for you?" she asked. "Like, what was the point?"

"Caroline wanted you... biddable." Lie. Caroline would have killed me if she'd known I'd put my filthy hands on Poppy's beautiful body. The order had been to keep her safe. And to keep my distance.

"And she thought sex with you would make me biddable?"

"You being preoccupied with me made you biddable."

"But you kept telling me to leave? What part of the job was that?"

"It wasn't," I answered and watched her eyes go wide.

"This isn't part of the job, either, is it? This cottage. Being here?"

"It would be safe to say I am no longer employed by Caroline Constantine." In the mad run from New York to this place, I hadn't actually thought that before. I'd betrayed the one person I'd sworn never to betray and there would be a reckoning. That was how it worked. And whatever I fucking felt about that, I put away. Far away.

"Why won't you fuck me?"

The question knocked me sideways for a second. "You asked your questions, Poppy. It's my turn."

"Right," she said with a sharp laugh. "The game. It's always a fucking game with you."

I crossed the small bathroom and braced my hands on the tub beside her body. She looked up at me, the balance of the scales between us shifting—more fear than arousal.

"It's business, Poppy. Not a game."

"What's the difference?"

"In my business? Life or death."

She lifted her hand and touched my face, the scar beneath my chin, and I was tired, so goddamned tired, that it was the only reason I let her. The only reason I stood there and soaked up her touch like sunshine after a long night.

"You're in a bad business," she whispered, her slick fingers touching the corner of my mouth, pulling at my lip. I gave her what she wanted, which was to be inside me. The only way I was ever going to let her. I sucked her finger into my mouth and watched her eyes go wide, then half-lidded, instantly drunk on our chemistry.

There. That's where I want you. Where I need you.

CHAPTER SIX

Ronan

I PULLED BACK. "We're partners now," I told her, my voice low, my eyes locked on hers. This was a tightrope I did not like, holding myself distant while pulling her in.

"Fine," she said. "Partners. But don't lie. No more lying."

"The same to you, Poppy."

She nodded, her breath hitching with nerves and desire. "Ask your question."

I sat on the edge of the tub. "Why would the Morellis want you dead or alive?"

"How do you even know this? Like, is there some kind of bad guy newsletter you're all on and you get updates about murders for hire?"

I would not smile at her. Would. Not.

"It's what Theo said before I put a bullet in his brain."

"Did you kill him for shooting me?"

"I'm asking the questions now. Why do the

Morellis want you dead or alive?"

I saw it settle over her face. The confusion and fear. "I'm no one. Nothing."

You're not no one, I wanted to tell her. *And you are far from nothing.* But how I felt about her was never the point. "Well, that's what we need to figure out, Poppy. And fast."

"Okay," she whispered, nodding, a star pupil. "What do we know about the Morellis?"

"They don't hide their crimes. Of which there are plenty. They're as rich, if not richer, than the Constantines."

"That must bother Caroline."

"Everything about the Morellis bothers Caroline."

"She doesn't want me dead or alive, does she?" Poppy asked, like the question was pulled from her stomach.

"She very much wants you alive. And living in her pocket."

"I guess . . ." She blew out a slow breath. "I was an idiot thinking she loved me. That we were family."

"Oh, princess, she treats everyone like that. It's not just you." I'd known going in I was a tool for Caroline. A weapon she wielded against her enemies. But at the beginning, being needed that way, and being appreciated in any way... well, it'd felt like love. Like a mother's love. To a killer who didn't know his mother, Caroline had filled those shoes in a way that embarrassed me now.

But I wouldn't be saying any of that out loud.

"What do you know about the Morellis, Poppy?" I asked, pushing us back to the subject at hand.

"They're violent," she said. "Lawless. Like... they don't play by the same rules Caroline and her family play by."

"They don't care about the same things. But," I said. "They're upfront about it. The Constantines are a knife in the back. The Morellis are a gun to your face."

"You sound like you admire them."

"They're a worthy enemy, and I spent a lot of years fighting them. Did Caroline ever tell you anything about them? Something that might have seemed like a secret?"

"Never. I swear it. She rarely talked about them. I don't even know what the feud is about."

"Money. It's always about money. And control. It started in the '50s over a land dispute in Las Vegas. Bryant Morelli and Caroline Constantine just inherited the fight."

"Would they want to hurt me because of

you?" she asked, pink cheeked and embarrassed. "Like, maybe they thought what was between us was real. On your end."

Ah, she was still wrestling with that bit. Fair. I was too.

"No one gives a shit about me."

"I do," she whispered. So sweet. So precious and sweet and brave sitting there.

I stood, getting some distance from the beautiful naked woman in the tub. "It's got to have something to do with the senator."

"I don't know what," she said.

"Yeah. Me neither." I sat down on the closed toilet lid and grasped a corner of the tray still balanced on the sink. "You want some of this?" I asked her. "You must be starved."

"I don't want to get crumbs in the bathtub. But I can't..." She sighed and gave me a chagrined smile. "I can't actually get out of the tub. My arm..."

Pulling her up and out of the water was nothing. Resisting the press of her body against mine was harder. She was damp and warm and soft against me.

"Here," I breathed, looking away from her face and sweeping her legs up over the edge of the tub. I set her down on the mat and I made the mistake of looking into her deep brown eyes.

With my blood-soaked killer hands, I touched her throat, the fragile edge of her collarbone, the sensitive skin of her neck where she'd been bruised that day when I saw her in her kitchen. It had been easy, for the two years when I didn't cross paths with Poppy again, running Caroline's obstacle course, earning her approval crime by crime, to believe Poppy wasn't getting hurt by her husband. I'd known, of course, the second I met the guy just what kind of man he was. How he shared the same space as the priests up the hill in the school I'd been sent to.

But then she'd stood in that kitchen, trying to make awkward small talk with me, worrying the cuff of her sweater and pulling the neck aside until I saw that bruise. After that, there'd been no more pretending. If I could have, I would have turned right around and put a bullet in that man's brain that very minute.

But I'd been a beast on a leash.

I set Poppy away from me and grabbed a towel hanging by a hook on the back of the door to wrap it around her. She was shivering now in the cooling air. Hungry no doubt. "Come on," I said. And with the tray in one hand and my other arm around her, I led her out of the bathroom and into the room with the fire. I pushed the chair up close to the hearth and sat her down in it.

"I'll get the chair wet," she said, her hair streaming down her back.

"It'll dry. Eat." I pressed the butter-covered bread I'd made for her into her hands. I poured her a cup of tea, putting plenty of sugar and milk in it, and set it on the tray so she could reach it.

I made myself the same and dug in.

She made a low moan of pleasure and I remembered, when I didn't want to, Sinead feeding me the exact same all those years ago. Sweet, milky tea and butter an inch thick on fresh bread. It was proper medicine.

"Was there something from the senator's will?" I asked. "Anything surprising, like?"

"That he left it all to me," she said, licking her lips and leaving them shiny. "I'm rich now. Like . . . really rich."

I shook my head, sitting back with my own cup of tea, wishing it was coffee. "The Morellis wouldn't kill you for a couple of million dollars. That's nothing to them."

Poppy pouted at me and it was ludicrous, but so undeniably . . . cute.

"Are you mad because I don't think your fortune is big enough?" I asked her.

"Maybe."

I laughed, a low surprising rumble from the center of my chest, and the sound startled us both. Her eyes lit up like the sunrise, and, uncomfortable, I turned away.

"You know," she said after a long moment. "I thought it was really weird that he used the lawyer he did. He was local out of Bishop's Landing. Why wouldn't he use some multimillion-dollar firm out of New York City?"

"That is weird," I said.

"And." She looked at me, the fire reflected in her eyes. "There was a box of stuff he gave me. Files from a trust he'd been creating and some things to do with the foundation . . ."

I got to my feet. "Why didn't you tell me this earlier?"

"Because I didn't know if we were on the same side earlier. You locked me in my room."

"Where's the box?"

"Still at the house. I was looking at it when Theo came in. I shoved it under the desk but . . . wouldn't the police have found it when they found Theo's body?"

"Theo's body wasn't at your house." Theo's body was buried in the Ocean City Landfill. Another favor I called in.

The truth was Caroline had probably been through that house in the hours I'd been gone with a fine-tooth comb. At this point, I had no friends in the Constantine house. But I might have some at the police department.

And I had one favor left. My last ace card.

My plan could backfire spectacularly. Or it could be a moot point. But the box was the first solid clue we had.

I stood and pulled Sinead's landline out of the cupboard where I'd hidden it when we first got here.

"You hid the phone from me?" Poppy asked.

"I'm trying to keep you safe."

"I don't think your 'safe' means the same as it does to me."

"What do you think it means to me?"

"Prisoner."

No matter how much I liked this sassy version of her, I would not smile. She needed no encouragement.

I plugged the phone into the jack and tapped the button under the receiver until I got a dial tone.

"Who are you calling?"

"I think I have one friend left," I said. "Who might be able to get the box without letting anyone know."

"Who?"

I glanced up at her. Like the people I knew were the people she knew. She traveled with minnows and I circled with sharks. "You don't know her."

"Her?" She couldn't hide her jealousy and I did nothing to ease it.

"Yeah," I said. "Her."

✧ ✧ ✧

Poppy

It never occurred to me that Ronan would have a... girlfriend? Was that the right word? Would a man like him have a girlfriend? The word seemed far too tame for the kind of woman he'd keep around in his life. Lover? Even that seemed ridiculous.

A wife? Oh my God. Was that why he wouldn't actually sleep with me? He could fuck around with me but not sleep with me because that was his moral marriage code? He turned away from me and I looked into the fire, pretending to give him privacy while I was actually listening as hard as I could to his side of the conversation.

He said something I couldn't understand, and it took me a second to realize he was speaking

Irish.

And as much as I wanted it to be extremely unlikely that Ronan had someone else in his life, the way he was talking to the woman on the other end of the phone was . . . well, it wasn't the way he talked to me, that was for sure. His tone was sweet. And kind.

I watched him for another second as he turned sideways, his profile so handsome and sharp it sliced right through me. And then, exhausted and full from the bread and the tea, I stood and went to the bedroom. I dropped my towel and climbed damp and shivering into the bed. Jealousy curdled in my stomach.

When I woke up, it was dark outside the small window and the door to the main room was open, the fire visible. There was a quiet roar that took me a second to identify as the shower running in the bathroom. I only figured that out when it suddenly turned off. A few seconds later, Ronan stepped out into the bedroom from a cloud of soap-smelling steam.

"Ronan?" I whispered.

"I didn't mean to wake you up," he whispered back, like other people were sleeping nearby when it was really just us and a lonely priest for miles.

"You didn't. What time is it?" Time was slippery right now.

"Nine. This is our second night here. You all right?'

He stepped forward and the shadows and light slipped over his bare chest. His stomach. His naked arms and shoulders. He had a blue towel with white flowers all over it wrapped around his waist, and water dripped from the tips of his hair onto his skin, dripping from the scar along his jawline onto his chest snaking paths over muscle and scars across his chest and stomach.

I'd never seen him naked, despite what we'd done together, which made him, in this moment, somehow more naked.

And so very beautiful. Every curve of muscle and ridge of bone was something I wanted to take in. To stare at and admire. There was a scar over his chest, a bright star fire. Another slice along his ribcage, catching just the edge of his abdomen. He looked both incredibly hard and infinitely soft. A blade and a feather. He was every contradiction. All I wanted in this world was to figure him out.

And touch him. I really, really wanted to fucking touch him.

"Poppy?"

"I'm fine."

"Your shoulder?" He kept getting closer to the bed, and I wanted to tell him to stop. To just give me a second. "You slept through your last dose. Let me get the meds."

"You're watching me sleep?"

He turned, and his back was a wide slope, curling in at his spine. The towel slipped as he walked, revealing the two dents at the top of his ass. I moaned, closing my eyes.

Naked in the bed, my skin felt alive, my blood humming just under the surface.

"Here," he said, bringing in a glass and shaking out the pills from the bottles on the bedside table. I waited for him to set the pills down on the counter, but he held them out to me, and I was forced to take them from his hand. His touch an electrocution. I bit my tongue against a gasp.

I put the pills on my tongue and drank the water he handed me, and he stood there watching me like a half-naked doctor. Beneath the thin towel around his waist, I could see the imprint of his dick, and the intimacy of it all was going to kill me.

"Where are you sleeping?" I asked. "Is there another bedroom?"

He shook his head. "I'm out there."

"You don't have to—"

"I don't sleep much, Poppy," he said. "It's fine."

I wanted to ask a million questions, but I kept them all behind my teeth. "Your friend? Is she able to get the box?"

"If it's there, she'll get it. She has a connection at the police station too. So, if they have it, she might be able to get it from them."

Oh, what a thing it must be to have Ronan's faith so securely like that.

"It never occurred to me that while we were . . ." Oh God, what was the right word? Not sleeping together? There was no right word for what had been between us. It certainly wasn't a relationship. It was barely a fling. But it was still somehow completely more consuming than all of that. "*You know* . . . you might have someone else . . . in your life. And I think . . . I think I deserve to know that. To know what I was a part of."

"You're asking if putting my mouth on your cunt was a betrayal of another woman?"

I could hear that ripple of laughter under his words. "Yes." I sounded prim to my own ears.

"You're thinking the woman I called to find the box was my missus?"

"Or something like that."

"Princess." He set down the pill bottle and braced his hands on the headboard over my head. I could smell the freshly washed scent of him. The bow of his arm muscle and the dip where it turned into his shoulder were close enough, should I choose to, I could turn my head and bite him. Looking at the black patch of hair in his armpit made me feel like he'd been kissing me for hours.

"Niamh is my landlady."

My eyes flew to his only to find him laughing at me. "You don't live at Caroline's?"

"She keeps her pets in her house. Not her monsters."

"You're not—"

Ronan talked over me. "Niamh had to leave the United Kingdom in 1982 or be tried for treason. Made her way to New York City and rents out part of her place to good Northern Irish lads like me."

"Ronan!"

"I'm serious." He was smiling again, almost laughing, and in all this time with him, I'd never seen him so relaxed. "She's seventy-two years old and can handle herself if anyone gives her trouble." He tilted his head; he was so beautiful when he smiled. It was hard not to smile back. It was hard, actually, not to put my arms around his neck and pull him down to kiss me.

God, I wanted him to kiss me.

"Were ya jealous, macushla?"

His accent was so thick I couldn't understand what he was saying. "What—?"

"Were you jealous, princess?" he asked, clearly this time, dropping some of what he'd said. "Thinking I was putting my tongue in another woman's cunt?"

I started to shake my head, not wanting to give him that much knowledge. That much power over me.

"I thought we weren't lying to each other anymore." He cupped my face, his thumb at my lips, forcing me to meet his eyes. "So?"

"Yes," I whispered. Caught. Immobile. "I was jealous."

"It was only you," he said. He brushed his thumb over my lips and then stood. I grabbed his hand before he could step away. This was ridiculous. I was... ridiculous. It was like standing in line to get knocked down and then, after getting knocked down, getting back in line to do it again.

Why did I want this pain so much? Why was I begging for him to hurt me?

"Poppy," he breathed. I saw his dick twitch beneath the towel, push against the white flowers. I put my hand over him, my fingers curling under the edge of the frayed fabric. He hissed in a breath like I burned him, and I liked it. I wanted that same fire to burn me.

With my fingers around his wrist, I pulled him closer, putting his hand under the blankets over the beat of my heart. His fingers were cold against my warm skin.

And he didn't stop me. Not even a little.

"All this talk," I said, "of cunts and tongues . . ."

His laughter was a solid bark of delight and I smiled in reaction. What a pleasure it was to please this man, and I wanted more. I pulled the towel out of the way, and his gorgeous cock was getting thick and hard right in front of my eyes.

I pushed his hand further down my body, over my breasts, down the smooth soft skin of my belly, while I reached for his cock.

"No," he said, shifting away from my touch.

"Why?"

"It doesn't matter why."

I tried to wiggle away, push his hand off my body, but he was steadfast.

"I don't want you touching me," he said. "But

I still want to touch you. You want me to stop?" His hand curled over my thigh and down between my legs. "You're wet, Poppy, but the words matter."

"They didn't before," I whispered, remembering the way I'd asked him to stop, and he'd pushed aside those words like they'd been made of paper and feathers.

He was silent, offering no other explanation. But if I said no, he'd walk away.

My whole body hurt with hunger for him. For the sweet violence of his touch. For the way he swept my mind clean.

And Ronan walking away was the last thing I wanted.

"Yes," I moaned, and the word was barely out of my mouth before his fingers slid down through the slick flesh of my pussy into the heart of my body. I bowed up off the bed, invaded and overrun by his touch. By the enormity of him. By the enormity of what I wanted.

Everything. I wanted every-fucking-thing.

He pulled the blankets off my body with his free hand before claiming my breast with his rough touch. I put my hands against the headboard and pushed myself down onto his fingers between my legs.

He made some rough growl in his throat. "Yes, princess. Use me. Use my fingers."

His thumb found my clit and he brushed it, barely touching it.

I shook my head. "More."

"I can't give you more. There is only what you take, princess."

I sat up and curled my hands over his cock. "This," I hissed into his face, drawn and bright with tension and lust.

"No." He smacked my hand away. "You can't have that."

"Fuck you," I grunted and lay back down against the warm sheets, his fingers still fucking inside of me. "Give me another finger," I demanded, and felt the push and stretch of him adding another. My eyes rolled back in my head.

"So full," he breathed. "So fucking beautiful."

I'd never in my life felt beautiful. Not on my wedding day. Not on any of those nights when so many people were paid to make me look as good as possible. I didn't know how beautiful felt, so there never seemed to be a way to look beautiful. Not for me.

But this moment changed that.

I did feel beautiful, naked and fucking myself on his fingers. My hands cupping my tits. This was beauty. He and I together. This pleasure.

I grabbed him by the back of his head and pushed him down. He went, giving me a little resistance even as he laughed because that seemed to be the game now.

"What are you takin', macushla?"

"Your mouth," I said, and he fell on me, sliding his body between my legs. The hand that wasn't all but fully inside of me swept under my body, holding me still in the grip between his forearm and bicep.

There was no careful seduction. No soft licks. None of that. He *devoured* me. He pushed the whole of his face against my clit. He sucked hard and I exploded in orgasm, grabbing his head with both hands as I ground myself into him. Onto him. Through him if I could.

Tears suddenly bit at my eyes and I couldn't blink them back in time. He lifted his face and saw me in the half-light. I wiped away the tears while he watched, feeling more naked now than I did two seconds ago.

"Are you okay?"

"Fine."

"Your shoulder?"

"Yeah," I lied. "But it's all right."

He climbed up my body, his legs on either

side of my hips. His cock stretched up nearly to his navel. Come oozed out the tip and I watched, wide-eyed, as he palmed his cock and squeezed it, groaning in his throat.

"Let me," I whispered, trying to sit up to put my mouth on him.

"No," he said, pushing me gently back on the bed. "Like this."

Like what? I wondered, lying beneath him, restless and aching again for more just at the sight of him jacking himself.

"You were teasing me in the bath," he murmured, his fingertips gently brushing my breasts. He stroked me from the top of my breasts to the curve near my armpit and around to press his hand flat on my chest between my breasts. "Weren't you?"

"I didn't think you noticed," I said. "Or cared."

"I notice everything about you," he said. "You have beautiful breasts, Poppy."

"They're not—" I stopped, shaking my head, not wanting the senator's voice anywhere near here.

"What?"

"Nothing." I kept my lips shut. If there were parts of himself he was keeping separate, there were parts of me I could keep back too. I didn't owe him all my pain.

He smiled at me like he knew what I was doing and approved of it. "Cup your breasts, Poppy." He briefly took my hands and covered my breasts. I pushed them up for him to see. The hand around his cock started to move. Harder. Faster.

"You want a show?" I whispered, arching like an actress in the porn I'd watched in the early days of my marriage trying to understand what the senator might want.

"I want to fuck them," he growled.

I blinked, taken aback. I knew it was a thing but didn't know how. My breasts were small. Hardly . . . fuckable.

"God, look at that face. Look at all that innocence. It makes me want to defile you, princess. Ruin you. It makes me want to fuck—"

"Do it," I said. "Just . . . fucking do it." I was beyond submission at this point. I was sharp toothed and feral with desire. He could do whatever he wanted to me.

He reached behind his body, slipping his fingers between my legs, and I moaned, arching into the contact. But he only took his fingers, damp with my come, and smeared it over my breasts.

He leaned forward, touching the tip of his cock to my nipple, and I swear to God that shouldn't have felt so electric. But it was like every nerve ending began and ended in that tiny touch. His hand cupped my breast, pushing it up at the same time he spat into his other hand, rubbing it on his cock. He was crude and vile and I loved it.

"You're so soft, Poppy," he said. "You're the softest thing I've ever touched."

I pressed my breasts together, cradling his cock between them. He pressed his hand down flat against his cock, and I arched. He pressed more, and it was clumsy and hot. His face as he watched his cock on my body was the most erotic thing I'd ever seen. He was transfixed, his lips parted, his cheeks flushed.

I moaned, wanting more. Wanting him inside of me. And he pressed forward more, one hand braced against the wall.

"Look at you," he kept saying. Over and over again. His eyes half-lidded, every muscle in his body flexed and then relaxing.

"You're so beautiful," I said, and then wished I hadn't. Too much. I couldn't give this man too much because he would take it all.

He bowed his head, his dark hair hiding his

face, and he palmed his cock and worked himself over harder. Faster. "Fuck... yes!" He groaned, and then come erupted from his cock, landing hot and damp against my chest and stomach. The corner of my mouth.

Maybe it was the front-row seat—I had no idea—but I'd never felt like this before. So out of control and needy. With trembling fingers, he reached out and stroked the come into my skin. He touched my lip and I licked him off.

"You shouldn't let me do this to you," he whispered, rough and ragged.

Oh God, the things I would let this man do to me.

"You're probably right," I murmured instead. Again, he smiled at me. "But I don't want to stop. I want more... I want more, right now."

He licked his lips and pushed back his hair with both hands. Watching me with dark glittering eyes. I felt seen. All the way down to my bones. I could say anything I wanted to this man, any crude and cruel thing that came to mind, and he wouldn't judge me for it. How freeing it was. I had to put on my best self for every other person in my life. The version of me with the smoothest edges and the brightest smile.

If I growled at Ronan, he growled right back.

"Touch me," I whispered. "Make me come again."

"Who made you so greedy?"

"You did."

His smile was wicked. "I like that too much, princess. I like touching you too much. I like making you scream too much."

"I like all of that too," I confessed, ready for the screaming and the touching. My hands ran up and down his thighs and I watched his dick get harder the more I touched him. But then suddenly he was off me, leaving cold behind him.

"What?"

"This isn't going to happen again, macushla. I didn't bring you here for this."

I sat up in the bed as he grabbed the towel and wrapped it around his waist. "Why did you bring me here."

"To keep you safe."

I shrugged. "We can't have both?"

Even as I asked the question, I saw his answer. He was too well conditioned. The lessons of his youth were embedded in his brain. He could not have both and since he couldn't... he would choose my safety.

Fuck. I felt that dangerous tilt in my chest. The loosening of my guards. The crumbling of my defenses—which, I could be honest, were pretty shit defenses when it came to this man. I'd let him storm me all day long.

"You can watch," I said and ran my hands down my breasts, over my belly, smearing his come into my skin. "That would be all right, wouldn't it?"

He was silent. And he didn't move. So, I put my hand between my legs and closed my eyes.

"I'm pretending it's you," I moaned and touched myself the way he touched me. Hard and relentless and without any shame. He stayed in the room. I could feel his eyes on my body, like the fire in the other room. And in the silence after my orgasm, I heard the creak of the door as he left.

CHAPTER SEVEN
Ronan

YOU KNOW WHAT'S too fucking small? A one-bedroom gaff. Particularly when Poppy, who was a different kind of Poppy from the young scared lass in New York, was in the bedroom. I felt her there like a throb in my dick.

I'd made right bags of everything.

I got dressed in front of the fire, finally using the clothes Sinead had left me, which were warm and clean and felt good on my skin after too many days in my own destroyed clothes. I ate some turkey and the last of the bread, and I then started to make my list.

The What the Hell Are We Going to Do Next? list.

Poppy needed a new identity and a new passport to support it.

Pray to God Zilla was at my safe house in London and I could get Poppy there without incident. Poppy would need cash because all the wrong people would have trip wires all over her bank accounts.

And once ID and money and Zilla were sorted, the plan was for Poppy to get as far away from me as possible. The sisters could hide out in Europe for a year. Or two.

And I would go back and kill every person who wanted Poppy hurt.

Even Caroline.

Especially Caroline if it came to that.

There was a knock at the door, unexpected but somehow not. I pulled my gun from where I'd put it on the mantel and walked silently to the door. Using the barrel of the gun to lift the curtains away from the side window, I wondered what kind of assassin just knocked on the front door.

Caroline, I thought. But I'd never told her about this place. That was why I'd brought us here.

I'd only ever told Poppy.

But it wasn't Caroline standing there. It was Father Patrick looking very nervous.

Fuck. I'd forgotten the father and Poppy giving him Zilla's number. I was tired and my thinking was shite.

I opened the door, making no effort to hide

the gun in my hand. A cat, the cat Poppy had talked about, ran from whatever hidey-hole it had been in and out the door.

"The fuck you want?" I asked the priest in the traditional greeting of my people.

"Ronan," he said and then stopped, probably all out of courage.

"Yeah?"

"I just . . . I'm checking on the lass. On you and the lass. I just want to make sure everyone is all right, like?"

"We're fine," I said, about to close the door.

"No. Stop—" He surprised both of us by sticking his arm out so if I did slam the door, I'd break his arm. Which wasn't such a deterrent. But he had a blue file folder in his hand. Which was weird.

I eased open the door, my eye on the folder. The hair on the back of my neck stood on end. "What is that?" I pointed the gun at the folder.

"I'll tell you," he said. "But I'd like to see your wife first."

I laughed in Father Patrick's face. "Look at you, playing the tough." He stared me down and I had to give the man a little bit of credit. Here he was hours too late to do any good, but pretending to be courageous? That was exactly the way I remembered him.

"She's sleeping. I'll give her your regards."

"You're not really married to her, are you?"

"Sure, we are." I didn't bother to make it sound like the truth. I smiled into the roar of silence between us, but he only lifted his chin, calling my bluff.

"I texted her sister at that number."

Jesus.

"Did she answer?" I asked. *Please, God. Please tell me she didn't fuckin' answer.*

"No."

I blew out a long breath of air. That was something, at least. One thing breaking my way. Not that I deserved it, forgetting like I did that Poppy had asked the priest to reach out to Zilla.

"Not yet," the priest added.

"What did you tell her?"

"That her sister was safe. That she was in a village outside of Carrickfergus."

There were a hundred villages outside of Carrickfergus. If the wrong person was on the other end of that phone, they'd still have work ahead of themselves to find us. But they'd know where to start. The window I had opened getting Poppy out of the country and away from the people who wanted her dead or alive was closing. The clock was ticking. I needed to get my shit together and fast.

"Listen . . . if someone does get back to you, you need to tell me."

Father Patrick smiled at me sadly. "I'll tell her, son—"

"I'm not your fucking son," I snarled.

"Sorry," he said. "Part of the job, I suppose. Everyone is a child of the Lord in my eyes."

"I'm not a child of anything." I stepped back, starting to close the door again.

"Just a second, Ronan." Father Patrick held out the file. "I wanted to give you this."

I wasn't touching that thing with a ten-foot pole. "What is it?"

"It took me a second to realize you might have been a student at the school. When I went to town, I spoke with Sinead who told me you weren't Ronan Smith, but Ronan Byrne. You're the boy who—"

"What the fuck's in the file?" I interrupted, not needing any reminders of what I'd done or why I'd done it.

"When they closed down the school and sent Father McConal away, we were told to destroy the files."

"Whose files?"

"The students."

"The prisoners, you mean?"

Father Patrick nodded. "I suppose. Yes. That might be a fitting word. But I couldn't... I couldn't destroy them. The church was burying what had happened at St. Brigid's, and it felt like burning the files would have been more of the same. And it just didn't seem right."

"So, you've been handing them out?

"Some of the boys who stayed local, I found them and gave them back."

"That must have gone well." I laughed, imagining with delight how Tommy might have responded to the return of the file if he'd actually been able to survive what they'd done to him.

Father Patrick touched the ridge of his nose, which looked like it'd been smashed once or twice before. "I don't have any way of making things right. Of making what happened in the school before I got there... right."

"Don't fucking absolve yourself, Father. You took your time reporting what happened. And if it wasn't for Sinead, you never would have done it."

"Don't sell yourself short, boyo," he said. "You're the one who lit the match."

"Pikey Tom lit the match," I snapped. In the

wake of my fury, Father Patrick made a sign of the cross, which made me want to murder him where he stood.

I had to hand it to the fucker. He looked ready to take whatever I was going to throw at him, and I again felt the reinforcement of what I had been taught to be true. There was no benefit to weakness. There was no comfort in it, no strength. Weakness was only rewarded with pain. Loathing.

And this guy, despite his effort at strength right now, was full of loathing.

"I know it's no excuse," Father Patrick said. "But I didn't realize how bad it was and once I did . . . I confess, to my shame, that I didn't want to believe it to be true. I hesitated doing what I knew needed to be done. And for that, I'll spend my life asking forgiveness from the Heavenly Father and all the boys at the school. Especially Tom."

Stupidly, I thought of those three months between the moment I knew Poppy was being abused by the senator and the moment I put a bullet in his head. Three months.

Hesitation had its own shame.

"So?" I asked, looking down at the blue folder. "What's in there?"

"Your criminal record. Birth record. School too. Hospital."

"I bet that was good reading."

"I haven't read it, Ronan. I'm just trying to give it back to you."

"What the fuck is that supposed to do?"

"I don't know. Give you some peace. Some closure."

I grabbed the file out of his hands and took two steps back to the fireplace, tossing the folder into the embers there. "There," I said. "You gave it to me. Now go feel your shame back in the church. And Father, for your own good, don't come down here again."

Father Patrick wasn't much older than me and I'd known plenty of boys from the neighborhood who'd picked a collar as a way out of the crime and poverty. There was a sense that we might have known each other at a different time. A different way.

"Ronan. If you ever feel the need to confess your sins—"

I shut the door in his face.

Behind me there was the pop in the fireplace, and I turned to see the blue edge of the file folder start to go brown and then black as it smoldered.

I'd never seen my file. Any of those files. The

hospital records I'd lived through. I had no interest in revisiting split lips and bruises across my shoulders. And school, well, caring about Maths and Geography was a luxury I'd never had.

But the birth record was . . . interesting.

My ma's name was Gwen. That was all I knew of her, really. That and she'd died just after I was born. A massive hematoma, bleeding to death before the doctors could save her. It didn't matter—her last name or where she was from. I mean . . . what could it possibly matter?

It didn't. It didn't fucking matter.

Before the whole thing went up in flames, I grabbed it out of the fire. Dropped it on the wood floor and stepped on what was burning.

I could see, just under the ragged burnt edge of the folder, my intake photo in Derry when I'd gotten pinched for taking the car. And then punching a constable. Fourteen years old and so mad. So fucking mad. What a gobshite I was. A total prick. But that rage had been the key to survival.

Looking at that picture and the bruises around those furious eyes felt like someone was walking across my grave. So, I picked up the folder and set it on the mantel, the picture turned away from me.

CHAPTER EIGHT
Poppy

I WOKE UP slowly. Sweetly, almost. It was completely decadent to be naked in a cocoon of warm blankets. There was no spike of fear. No wave of worry. There was just asleep and then awake and memories of Ronan.

God. I was consumed by him. By his distance and his intimacy. Torn in half by what he gave me and how much more I wanted from him.

I pushed off the covers and pulled on the sweatpants and sweater that were folded on the foot of the bed. Whatever I was—prisoner, escapee—apparently, I didn't get underwear. I ran my fingers through my tangled hair as best I could and my shoulder was aching, so I slipped on my sling before stepping out into the main room of the cottage, braced for Ronan and his cold, slicing distance. But the main room was empty. The fireplace was cold. Rubbing my arms against the chill, I stepped into the kitchen and pressed my hands against the kettle. It was cold too.

"Ronan?" I called, not sure where he would be hiding in the tiny cottage. I looked out the window where the car had been parked yesterday, but there was only light gravel where it had been.

Gone.

Panic vanished just as quickly as it came. Ronan wouldn't go to all this work just to leave me here. Would he?

No. I decided no. He wouldn't.

The bread was gone so I grabbed a piece of turkey from the fridge and ate it before taking my antibiotic with a glass of water. I skipped the pain pills because they made me loopy, and the ache wasn't bad enough for all that. There was also a pot of stew and a jar of jam in the fridge. Some apples and wilted head of lettuce. Maybe he went into town to get groceries.

Suddenly, I had a picture of an oddly domesticated Ronan that didn't fit any part of what I knew about him. But truthfully, what did I know about him? Slightly more than nothing and half of that was lies.

The sun was butter yellow in a bright blue sky, and the grass was so green it didn't seem real. Up on the hill, I could see Father Patrick working in his garden and I wondered what part of Ronan he knew. What secrets the priest could unlock. Ronan would hate me talking to the priest. Hate me asking about him.

It wasn't decent. Or respectful. Or kind. But I wasn't feeling kind anymore. I felt like baring my teeth and getting answers.

I shoved my feet back in the boots I'd worn briefly yesterday and pulled open the door, letting in the cat that seemed to come and go as she pleased. I made sure she had food and tried to scratch her ears while she ate, but she hissed at me, claws extended.

"Sorry," I muttered, thinking this cat and Ronan had a few things in common.

I left and took the path around the cottage up the hill to the church. The wind and the sound of the waves roared around me, and Father Patrick didn't hear me until I was practically right beside him.

"Sorry, Fath—"

I'd spoken quietly, trying not to startle him, but he jumped anyway, bashing into a staked pea plant with tiny, curly tendrils climbing up a string tied to the fence.

"Jaysusmaryandjoseph!" Father Patrick yelled, a hand against his heart. "You scared me!"

"I'm sorry. I was trying not to."

"Everything all right?" he asked and then again more seriously, "are *you* all right?" He pointed at my sling.

"I'm fine. It's just a sore shoulder. Honestly. I just woke up and saw the sunshine and you in your garden, and thought I'd ask if you needed any help."

"Your husband would not like you being here."

"Well, my husband is not here at the moment and if he were—he's not the boss of me." Father Patrick barked a disbelieving laugh, and a blush heated my cheeks. "Would you like some help?"

"Well, I don't want to cause any trouble but . . . more hands make light work." He pulled the ball of string from the ground.

"Just tell me what to do," I said.

He explained how he was staking strings tied to the fence next to the pea plants so they could grow up the string. "I get more peas that way," he explained, and I began tying one end, holding the string taut while he cut and then staked the other end of the string. It was awkward with the sling, but I made it work.

"This is quite a garden," I said. It really was big. Organized and tidy.

"Thank you. A true labor of love."

"Has it always been here?"

He was silent and I looked down at him only to find him shielding his eyes as he looked at me. "I started it some years ago. With the help of two students from the school."

"Well, it's impressive. I can't keep a cactus alive."

"That's trickier than you think," he said. "Because they don't need much, you forget to give them anything and when they're dead, they still look like they're living."

"That's it exactly," I said with a laugh. And then realized that had been a pretty fitting description of my life before Ronan came in and blew it all up.

"I texted your sister," he said. I turned, having forgotten the problems that could cause, and my stomach went suddenly cold. "I didn't hear back from her."

"You shouldn't... you shouldn't do that again. I mean, I shouldn't have asked you to do it in the first place."

"Ronan told me. I understand. But I didn't want you to think that you'd asked and I hadn't done it."

"Thank you, that's kind of you."

"If I do hear from her, I'll let you know."

"Thank you."

"Your sister, what's her name?"

"Zilla."

"That's an interesting name."

"My mom said she wanted to call her Zinnia. After the flower. Poppy and Zinnia. But the nurse filling out the paperwork heard Zilla and wrote it down. I guess it just stuck."

Out of the blue, a wave of fear for my sister absolutely crushed me. Of worry. Of missing my sister. I pressed a hand to my chest and a sob hiccupped out of me. I bent my head, trying to get myself together.

"Lass, lass, what's gotten into you?" The priest abandoned the pea plants, the string falling into the dirt. Awkwardly, he patted my uninjured shoulder once and then sort of hovered.

"I'm sorry." I gave him a watery smile. "I just really miss my sister."

"You're close, then."

"Yes."

It was all I said because there was no explaining the bond I had with Zilla. There was nothing this pseudostranger could say and so he didn't try, returning to the pea plants. It was comforting to just work in silence.

"Do you have any siblings?" I finally asked.

"I am the youngest of four brothers," he said. "Each of us fewer than two years apart."

"Your poor mom."

"Indeed."

"So, Father, if you don't mind me asking, what made you decide to join the church?"

"It's not a very interesting story," he said. "I'd rather hear how you met your husband."

He looked up at me under his lashes, letting me know he didn't believe our story.

"You first," I said with a smile.

"Ma always wanted one of her sons to be a priest."

"Your other brothers weren't interested?"

"They were occupied."

"Having families?"

"Getting arrested."

I laughed before I caught myself and the priest smiled, pleased. "Two of them managed to straighten out and get married. Gave me four nephews and two nieces."

"The other one?"

"Died. In jail." He made a sign of the cross. "We grew up in a shite neighborhood. Council housing. Gangs. Bad schools. It was the kind of place that didn't want you to succeed, I reckon. And when I got the job as a teacher up here, I thought I would have something in common with those boys, but I'd been so green they just made meat out of me."

"Ronan grew up in the same kind of neighborhood. He told me when he was little, he wanted to be a priest because they seemed to have so much power."

"That's one way of looking at it," he said. "Where did you grow up? Not in the same neighborhoods as me and Ronan, I imagine."

"What makes you say that?"

"You got this . . . shine about you. This hope." He looked up at me, squinting against the sunlight. "Makes me think you grew up thinking you could do anything. Be anything."

"I did," I said, startled to realize, in a way, that was true. I was equally startled to realize I still had any innocence left. Perceived or not. I felt hard to the touch. Brittle all the way through. "Until I was eighteen. And then . . . my sister got sick, and everything sort of fell apart." I felt the ghostly grip of the senator's hands around my fingers.

"I'm sorry," he said.

"Me too, but . . ." I smiled again. "I did have a nice childhood, though. My sister and I both. We grew up by a pond and we had a lot of freedom and we had each other."

"I'm glad." He nodded and handed me the next end of string so I could tie it to the top row of the fence.

The black cat I'd seen the other day was prowling through the tall grass near the shed. It pounced on something and another cat jumped out of the grass to wrestle.

"There are a lot of cats around here," I said.

"There used to be a feral cat colony here years ago. Sinead saved three of them. One of them adjusted to living in her house but the other two keep coming back up here to sleep with my cow in the shed."

"What happened to the rest of them?"

"Father McConal had them killed some years ago. Said they were pests, and he was trying to prove a point."

"To who?"

"One of the boys who lived here."

"That's a mean way to prove a point."

"Yes. It was." He nodded and the conversation drifted into silence.

Within a few minutes, I'd tied the last of the string and he was brushing the loamy black dirt off his hands. Below us, there was still no sign of the car. I wasn't ready to go in yet. The sunshine was warm, the breeze was briny, and I felt better than I had . . . in ages.

"It's so pretty here, isn't it? Looks like a postcard."

"The church has offered to move me over the years. To someplace bigger with more people."

"You're not interested?"

"At first, I was worried that if I left, they wouldn't find someone to live here, and St. Brigid's deserves better than to be all alone. But now, it's my home and I couldn't imagine being anywhere else."

"It must be nice to know where you belong," I said, unable to hide the longing in my voice.

I braced myself for some platitude, some "Home is where the heart is" crap, but he only nodded and said, "It is."

It occurred to me, on this rocky edge of the world, that the only place that had ever really felt like home was that pond and the willow tree next to it when I was a kid.

It was the only place where I wasn't scared, and I could be myself. Inside the house, we'd all balanced on our tiptoes, afraid of our mother's mood swings and mental state. And the senator's house had been the opposite of a home. I'd renovated and decorated myself and my comfort right out of it.

Down there is nice, I thought, looking at the cottage and the man who'd brought me there.

But that was an uncomfortable thought too.

"It looks like your carrots could use some weeding," I said, pointing to the corner of the fenced-in garden where the feathery heads of carrots were just beginning to unfurl.

"You know." He laughed. "I've been waiting until the weeds got a little bigger because last year, I pulled out all the carrots and not the weeds. My eyes aren't as good as they used to be."

I started pulling one-handed, and he protested for a second but quickly gave up and went over to do some work with the tomato plants.

"You know, the fence is broken back here," I said. The chicken wire had been bent back and I tried to bend it forward again, but it was rusted from the salt air and stuck. He needed a whole new section of chicken wire.

"I know. The deer around here are very clever. The hole isn't big enough for them, but the pine martens are having a fine time."

"You need a dog?"

"A dog I would like," he said. "But the cats might not."

"Why don't you get one?"

"Not sure, to be honest. Not getting what I

want has become a very strange, very Catholic habit." He laughed when he said it, but he seemed so sad.

"I know that habit," I said. "And I'm not Catholic."

If I got out of this nightmare, what I wanted would be the only thing that mattered. I wouldn't be anyone's pawn, anyone's wife. I'd be me on my own. I'd finish my degree. I'd get in the classroom, and fuck anyone who stood in my way. Even thinking that made me feel better.

Braver.

"When I get back home," I said. "Nothing is stopping me."

"Good for you, lass," he said. "Perhaps I'll see about that dog."

I held out my left hand and he looked at me for a second and then laughed, a good hearty laugh. "We're shaking on it?"

"We're shaking on it."

Grinning at each other, we shook, and for all the lies and pretenses, it felt like we were friends.

"Well, Poppy, you've done all my chores," he said, his hands on his hips, a little twinkle in his eye. "What will I do with the rest of my hours?"

"We could fix this fence."

"Not today, lass. Are you hungry?" At the

mention of food, my stomach answered for me and he laughed. "Brilliant! It's such a nice day; I'll bring us a picnic."

"Let me help—"

"Sit, lass. Sit." And then he was gone, heaving open the heavy door and vanishing into the church.

The wind pulled at my hair and I remembered this trick as a girl: twisting my hair and tucking it into my shirt. I lay back against the green grass, a rock nudging me under my uninjured shoulder blade but not bad enough for me to get up.

"Taking a nap, are you?" the priest asked, coming back down from the church to sit next to me. He did it carefully, holding the tray he carried at the same time. There was egg salad flecked with black pepper and crackers with seeds and juicy slices of cucumbers. He pulled two brown bottles and a white cloth stained pink from his pocket.

"The first of the strawberries," he said, setting the cloth down on the stone between us. "They'll put a pucker on your face, but I can't resist."

I put one in my mouth and shook head to toe from its tartness. He laughed and twisted the top off one of the bottles before handing it to me. Sweet hard cider washed away the sour from the corners of my mouth.

The father dipped a cracker in the egg salad and then placed a cucumber slice on top before putting it in his mouth. He grunted and reached for another one. "Better get in there before I eat it all."

I did what he did and within minutes, the bowl of egg salad was done, and we were eating the last of the cucumbers. My cider bottle was empty, and I could feel the cider in my knees. The muscles in my face ached from smiling.

"Do you get lonely up here by yourself?" I asked.

"Sometimes," he said. "But Sinead is usually around for a cup a tea if I need to hear another voice. How about you, lass? Are you lonely?"

The question was startling, perhaps because I'd never thought about it before.

"I was married," I said. "And it was the loneliest thing I'd ever experienced. Even though I was never really alone." I didn't try to explain the spies the senator had, or the spies the Morelli family had. And, apparently, Caroline.

"Sounds like it was a bad marriage."

"It's the kind of marriage that cures you of marriage," I said with a laugh, surprised a little by how much I meant it. I would never marry again. No man would have that much legal, financial, and emotional control over me. There wasn't enough love in the world to change my mind.

"You're not really married to Ronan, are you?" he asked, the question coming out of the blue.

Oh man. I just totally blew the cover. "No, I'm not."

"Are you in trouble, lass?"

I took a deep breath and let it out, my body slumping. "At the moment, no. But in the large scheme of things?" I waved my hand, indicating the wider world. "Yes."

"Is Ronan . . . hurting you?"

"What? No. Not at all. Father Patrick—"

"Because I knew him as a boy."

"From the school?"

"He was wild and could be vicious, trying to survive and get by, but he was sweet too. They all were. They were just boys and they had sweetness—"

"He still is," I said, because the priest was nearly frantic. I put my arm around him, and he took a deep shuddering breath. "He can still be very sweet."

"He doesn't seem it."

"I know," I said. "But he's taking good care of me."

"Oh, you must think me some dodgy fool," he said, looking at me sideways. There was something about him that was old despite the fact he couldn't be that much older than Ronan. "I just . . . I never thought I'd see that boy again."

I swallowed. "What happened? I mean, he's told me a little, but I don't know how he left the school. Or why. And I really don't understand why he would bring me back here if all there are, are painful memories."

Father Patrick looked out at the endless horizon and shook his head. "No, lass. He wouldn't want me telling you. I was the villain in his story."

That answer was expected, and I patted him on the shoulder. "Well," I said. "For what it's worth, I think you're a terrible villain."

"He wouldn't say that. It doesn't take real cruelty to be a villain. Sometimes, it just takes cowardice."

Down the hill, a plume of brown dust was rising from the road, a blue car coming toward the cottage.

"He's back," I said.

"Lass, if he's scaring you or threatening you—"

"It would be a day ending in 'y,'" I said with a dramatic roll of my eye.

"You can come to me," he said. "If you have

to. I can keep you safe."

He couldn't, actually. What was coming after me was coming with guns. The reality of what I'd done made my stomach roll over. By asking him to text my sister's number, I'd brought danger right to his doorstep. And those church doors were thick, but they weren't bulletproof.

"We'll be gone soon, I imagine," I told him. "You don't need to worry about me. Ronan is keeping me safe."

Safe and at arm's length. I was standing in front of a door he kept shutting in my face, which, because I was a fool, only seemed to make me want inside even more.

I got to my feet, my body a little swimmy from the hard cider and the weeding I'd done. I'd protected my shoulder as best I could, but the dull ache from earlier was now sharper and I wanted one of those painkillers. "Talk to you later, Father Patrick. Maybe tomorrow we can fix that fence." Though I wasn't sure I would be here tomorrow. I wasn't sure I would be here in an hour.

"He won't like you spending time with me," Father Patrick said.

"He doesn't like anything," I said with a smile and headed back down the hill.

CHAPTER NINE

POPPY

THE CAR PULLED into the drive just as I was coming around the edge of the cottage.

"Welcome home, honey," I said cheerfully as Ronan got out of the small car. Frowning at me, of course.

"What the fuck are you doing up at that church?"

"Gardening and getting a little drunk."

His eyebrows went up at that and I kept my hands to myself with great restraint. Anytime this man showed me any emotion, it made me horny. "Where did you go?"

"The village." From the back seat of the car, he pulled out a few plastic bags.

"Let me help," I said, reaching my good arm out for one of the bags and he ignored me, walking into the cottage with all the parcels.

He set the bags down on the kitchen table and pulled out some toothbrushes.

"Oh, brilliant," I said and ripped one open. He didn't actually grin at me, but I could feel him wanting to grin. "What?"

"You sound proper Irish."

"What can I say? You're rubbing off on me."

I found the toothpaste in the bathroom and started scrubbing my teeth that felt like they had fuzz growing on them. Ronan followed. For a few minutes, we stood side by side in the bathroom, brushing our teeth and taking turns spitting in the sink.

The mundaneness of it all was a little surreal.

"You didn't happen to get any underwear, did you?" I asked him.

"No," he said. "I didn't realize you had none."

"I'll live."

Back in the kitchen, he took a few more things out of the bag. Coffee and a French press.

"Something smells delicious," I said.

"That bag." He pointed to another bag and inside of it was a giant bundle of newspaper. "I stopped by the chippy."

I peeled open the paper, revealing a giant heap of fries and two pieces of fried fish on top covered in salt and vinegar. "Oh my God," I said, putting one of the fries in my mouth. "That's good."

"Yeah?" He gave a half smile. "I remember the

chips being good, but you know how—" He took a fry, too, and nodded after a bite. "Nope. It's as good as I remembered."

He pulled an older model flip phone out of his bag.

"Where'd you get that?" I cried.

"It's a burner from the shops."

"Can I call my sister—?"

"I did already," he said. "No answer."

"That's . . ." The sinking feeling in my gut said that was bad, but I couldn't say it out loud.

"Not good or bad," he said quickly, his eyes on mine. "Don't read too much into it."

"Can you tell me where she is at least?"

"I have a house in London. No one knows it's mine."

"Why?"

"A guy I worked for before Caroline found me told the only way to stay alive was to have as many escape routes as possible."

"This house is your escape route?"

"One of them. One of the last ones."

I imagined a sad apartment in some high-rise building. Something small and anonymous.

I abandoned the fries and curled into one of the chairs in front of the cold and empty fireplace. Ronan kept putting things away. Milk in the fridge. A bottle of whiskey in the corner of the counter. I remembered how he'd built the fire yesterday and got on my knees to give it a try.

Kindling. A lit match.

"I reached out to a few old friends," he said.

"That sounds ominous." I blew gently, but only managed to blow out the tiny flame that had caught. I started again. Kindling. A match. A lighter breath this time. The twigs caught.

"You need a new passport. Driver's license. Fake names and information. You need to dye your hair and cut it."

"I don't have hair—"

"I bought some." He lifted a box of drugstore hair dye from a bag and set it on the table.

I added a larger piece of wood, blowing gently on the coals. The larger piece of wood caught. Even one-handed I was a fire-building natural.

"Poppy Maywell needs to disappear."

I turned to him, unaware I was smiling.

"I expected a fight," he said. "But you don't seem too upset?"

"I'm not. It's just hair, and . . . I mean . . . God, what a relief not to have the senator's last name and frankly, I'm okay not having my father's last name either. Do I get to pick?"

He was making coffee, pouring hot water into

his French press. "Sure. If you like."

"What are you going to choose?"

He shook his head. "My name will stay the same."

"Because you're a badass and you don't care who knows it?" The fire was going pretty good, so I sat back in my chair, curling my legs under me.

His lip kicked up. "Something like that. How much have you had to drink?"

"Just one cider. It was delicious."

"What else did the priest try and feed you?"

"Egg salad and cucumbers."

"I meant stories. What stories did he try and feed you?"

He sounded so dark and skeptical. So prepared to believe the worst about the man on the top of the hill. It seemed so unlikely. Father Patrick was such a sweet man. "He said he was the villain in your story."

"Did he now?"

"Is that true?"

"One of them. There have been plenty of villains."

He sat down in the chair beside mine. He wore a thick cream sweater with worn cuffs and a high collar. He looked like a sailor, home on leave. That, too, made me horny.

"He said you were wild and could be vicious but that you were sweet."

"Hardly sounds like me," he said.

"I think it sounds exactly like you." I reached out with my foot, thinking I could nudge his knee with my toe, but he was too far away, and I had scrunched down in my chair and stretched in a totally ridiculous position. I pretended to nudge him anyway, and all while he stared at me slightly bewildered and aghast.

I laughed at his expression, too happy from the sunshine and the work and the cider to be put off by him. He took a sip from his coffee cup.

"You drink a lot of coffee," I said. He was silent. "Do you ever sleep?"

"I do."

"Not much."

He ate some fries, then broke off a piece of steaming fish and ate it. "You want some of this?"

I shook my head, full from the peppery egg salad. "Is it because you have bad dreams?"

"Memories, Poppy. I have bad memories."

"Me too," I said, still slouched in my chair. For a second, the air in the room was heavy with all our bad memories.

"I'm excited about a new name," I said, shaking off the weight. "A new life. I mean, as long as my sister is safe. Why not start over? With the ID, I can go to school, right?"

"Aye," he said, cradling the small cup in his big hand. "You won't have access to your money for a while, but I'll leave you with enough that if you want to take classes, you can."

"That doesn't seem right, taking your money."

"Well, it's that or starve. Your choice." He shrugged like it didn't matter to him, but the corner of his mouth was lifted.

"Taking the piss, are you?" I asked, and his eyebrows went back up. God, surprising this guy was getting to be an addiction. "I could get a job."

"What kind of job have you ever done?" he asked.

I gasped, outraged. Real outrage. "I'll have you know I built a shower in my backyard."

"Really?"

"Really."

He grunted and ate more of the fish. I could feel his dubiousness.

"The real question," I said. "Is what should I change my name to?"

"That's the real question, is it?" He stood and put another log on the fire. I could easily get used to being cared for by grumpy Ronan.

"Do I go for something grand like Genevieve? My college roommate was Genevieve and she used to say it like she was French even though she was from Ohio."

"No, you do not go for Genevieve."

"I've never met a Jenny I didn't like."

"I could introduce you to a few who'd probably kick you across the room if you'd like that."

"No. I wouldn't like that."

He stood, the fire crackling behind him, a smile on his face.

"What name would you pick? I asked.

"Ronan."

"For me, Ronan. What name would you pick for me?"

He sat down and looked at me, his attention making me giddy and uncomfortable all at the same time. I made a show of it, sitting up and pressing down the sweater I wore. Flipping my hair back over my shoulders.

"You look like Poppy," he said and made it sound sweet. A compliment. "It's hard to imagine you as anything else."

"What was your mother's name?" I asked, and the warmth of the moment vanished immediately. Ice had replaced the air.

"What does that have to do with anything?"

"Just gathering names."

"Gwen."

"That's pretty—"

"You're not picking my mother's fucking name."

"I didn't say I was."

He sighed, his eyes darting up to the mantel. I turned to see what he was looking at. There was a vase with dried flowers, pictures of a blond girl growing up, and a blue file folder.

"What's wrong?" I asked.

He rubbed his face, digging at his eyes. "Nothing."

"Is there something—?" I stood, reaching for the folder.

"Bree," he said.

"I look like a Bree?"

"Bree was the first girl I ever kissed."

I laughed. "You want me to pick the name of the first girl you ever kissed."

"She was nice." He shrugged, the cocky fuck. Sitting there, smiling at me.

"Beth," I said. "I'll pick Beth. It was my mother's middle name."

"Solid name," he said and nodded like it was all decided.

In the quiet, he crumpled up the waxy paper

where the fish and chips had been.

"So?" I asked. "What are we going to do all day?"

"You will dye your hair and I'll wait for my friend to call me back."

"That's hardly going to fill the day. Father Patrick needs his fence repaired."

"No."

"Ronan—"

"No."

"Then you need to entertain me, I imagine," I said with a smile, my meaning, I felt, pretty clear.

"You want to play cards while you dye your hair?"

"Ronan!"

He shook his head at me, frowning. I gave him my best pout. He turned away, but not before I saw the smile he was trying to hide.

"I feel very safe, Ronan. I mean, if you're worried if we fool around, I'll feel less safe. I won't." He stood and threw the wax paper away. He really was killing me in that sweater. "Have you ever fooled around with a Beth bef—"

"Stop begging, Poppy. It's unbecoming."

I caught my breath. I knew what he was doing, but it didn't take the sting out of his words. How easily this man found my weakest point and how gleefully he pressed on it. He really was a bastard.

Carefully, I stood. "Go fuck yourself, Ronan," I said quietly and walked toward the bathroom. I didn't hear him until he had me by the elbow, turning me around. I pulled away, my arm rising to wipe that fucking smug look off his face, but he wrapped his arms around me so I couldn't smack him.

"I'm trying to do what's right, Poppy," he whispered into my hair. "And you make it so damn hard."

"You don't need to say those things anymore," I said.

"What things?"

"The things you say just to hurt me. You don't need to push me away. I know how this ends."

He brushed the hair off my face. "I'm trying to make it easier, I think."

"For me?"

"For me."

He kissed me and I would consider this later, how I handed him the tools to hurt me over and over again, but his kiss was impossible to resist. He walked me backward to the bed and I felt like I'd never been in danger like this before. Like if I moved wrong, he could take out my heart. Every bit of it.

He laid me down on the bed and stood over me.

"If you're going to leave, just leave," I said. "I'm tired of you."

"I'm not going to leave you." He pulled off his sweater, revealing his chest and the way his life had left its mark on him. Brutal scars and hard muscles. "And you're not tired of me. Not at all."

"Yes, I am. You're boring."

"That's not what you think when you're coming all over my face."

"It is. It's exactly what I think." I had no idea why I was doing this. Why I was pushing and pushing and pushing. I yawned. "I think I'll just take a nap—"

He grabbed the sweatpants I wore and yanked them off me. The fabric ripped. I shrieked in surprise. "Those are my only pants!"

"If I want you naked, you'll be naked."

"Oh my God." I rolled my eyes.

He put his knee on the bed. "What will I find between your legs?" he whispered.

I curled right up and put my hands over my body. "My dry, cold, bored vagina."

"I don't think so, Poppy. I think you're sopping wet. I think you're so hot you'll burn me. I think one touch, and you'll beg."

"One touch, and I'll fall asleep," I said, and when he touched my leg, I flipped over and scrambled for the other side of the bed, careful as I could be of my shoulder. Fruitless, but the fight was the point. He was hard under those dark pants, and between my legs, my desire hummed at a fever pitch.

"Oh no," he said and grabbed my leg, pulling me backward. My sweatshirt got pulled up and with my good arm, I reached for the far side of the bed, trying to claw myself away. But then he climbed up my legs and sat on the tops of my thighs and spanked me.

Hard.

"You motherfucker," I snapped, trying to buck him off.

"Keep fighting, Poppy. I do like it when you fight."

So, it would seem, by the energy I could feel in my clit, did I. I pressed my pussy down against the mattress and bit my lip against a groan.

His hands cupped the bottom of my ass and I felt absurdly vulnerable. And absurdly turned. I gave him another half-hearted buck, which only made him laugh.

"You have a beautiful ass, Poppy."

"Well, you can kiss it." I snarled.

And he did. My snarl turned to a gasp and then to a low, throaty animalistic sound as his soft lips, scratchy jaw, and damp breath all made their way across my skin, from the tops of my thighs to my lower back. Again, I pressed myself against the mattress, seeking pleasure.

"No," he said and curled his hands under my hip bones, lifting me off the mattress. "Not yet."

"Fuck you," I said, without any convincing heat.

The game was over. The game had been a stupid ruse, but to some degree, the game kept me safe.

He kissed my spine. Bit the left cheek of my ass. Then the right. I whimpered low and needy, trying to arch into him and the bed. His hand left my hip, pressing along my back to my shoulder blades, and finally grabbed a fistful of my hair.

The sting only added to everything.

He leaned up to whisper in my ear. "What do you want?"

"You."

"No, Poppy. You don't want me. You want to come."

"I want you to make me come."

He lay down over my body, his weight pushing me into the mattress. He kicked my legs out wide and I felt the scratch of his denim against my thighs. The heat of his naked chest against my back. The hard press of his cock against my ass.

"It's not . . ." I pushed down against the mattress and up against him. "It's not enough."

He muttered something against my ear, low and guttural, his own animal coming out. His hand squeezed between my body and the mattress, finding my open legs. My burning wet flesh.

"Fuck, Poppy." He groaned, like he was amazed by me. As much as I was amazed by him. "You feel so fucking good." He found my clit and performed his magic. Between his fingers and the mattress. The press of his body. The smell of his breath. The beautiful reality of him.

Of us.

And it was terrifying how much I felt.

"Fuck you," I said.

The sweet sound of his laughter in my ear sent me spinning into orgasm the way his feigned cruelty never could.

CHAPTER TEN

POPPY

HE ROLLED MY limp body, still twitching with orgasm aftershocks, into his arms. The silence was loaded and thorny. The game was over, and we couldn't get it back. We'd been pushed into new territory, and I waited with every breath for him to get up and leave.

But he didn't.

"What happened?" I asked, running my finger across a scar just south of his left nipple.

"Ran into a knife."

"Just ran into it?" I asked with a startled laugh.

He shrugged. "A fight at a pub. I didn't see the knife."

"These?" I asked, putting my hand over a constellation of scars on his forearm.

"Hot oil," he said. "Da tossed it at me." He lifted his arm to show me how he'd blocked his face.

"This one?' I asked, tracing a thin line just above his pants, low on his abdomen.

"Appendix."

"You are human."

"Did I tell you I wasn't?"

Oh God. I kissed him. Hard. Too hard, maybe, but I didn't know what to do with this pain. This longing. He met my ferocity with his own. I pulled back to breathe and he kissed my neck, his hand snaking down my body to between my legs, and I knew how this would spin out. Me on my back with him between my legs making me come until I cried, and Ronan holding himself so distant, he might as well already be gone.

Again.

"We're doing this my way," I said and started easing down the bed while he was still half on top of me.

"Poppy," he breathed.

"Fight me, and you can leave," I said, looking at him. He stared at me, his lips parted, his face still. Surrender was not in his nature, but I really had to insist.

Finally, he rolled onto his side and I rolled onto mine. I wanted this bed to have walls and a ceiling. I wanted it to wrap around us, cocoon us. I kissed my way down his chest, across every scar and ridge of muscle. I felt the fluttering of his heartbeat against my tongue. The rise and fall of his belly as he sucked in air. I ran my hands down his sides, and he flinched.

I looked up, scared I'd hurt him.

"Ticklish," he said. "Tell anyone and I'll kill you."

He smiled at me and I smiled back as I eased his pants down, his cock springing free into my hand.

"Has anyone ever told you, you have a really pretty cock?"

"No, Poppy. That's not a thing people say."

"I say it. You have a beautiful cock, Ronan Byrne." I leaned forward, licking the tip. Slipping my mouth around the head.

"*A chuisle,*" he breathed, his hands sliding into my hair to hold onto my head. I hummed in my throat, liking the way his voice broke.

Listening to the cues of his heartbeat, his breathing, I gave my whole body over to his. My mouth and my hands. Every groan and deeply uttered curse. The clench of his fingers in my hair. The curl of his body as he fucked in and out of my mouth. I felt all of it so deeply in my own body. When he came. His cock against my tongue grew impossibly hard and he jerked back, trying to come anywhere but inside of me, but I held on.

I would have this, at least.

At least, I would have this.

"Poppy," he said. Just that. My name. I heard his surrender. His regret. I wished we could have one without the other between us. That his pleasure could be pure. But Ronan was Ronan, and I could not change him.

"Shhh," I said. "Just . . . shhh."

I pushed myself up to face him, smiling because he was disheveled and clearly exhausted against the sheets. I lay down next to him and used my fingers to brush aside his hair. That he didn't shrug away indicated how tired he was. His eyelids dropped and then opened wide. "Hey," I whispered. "How about you take a nap."

"Someone's got to be awake."

"I can be awake. You sleep, and I'll look out for you."

"You need to dye your hair."

"I can do both. I am an excellent multitasker."

Suddenly the cat leaped on the bed, looking at us as if she very much disapproved of our actions. "Jaysus!" Ronan muttered. "Where the hell did the cat come from?"

"I think she lives under the bed. The cat and I will look after you."

"You're ridiculous, Poppy."

I kissed his cheek. "The name is Beth."

"Never. Always Poppy to me."

The cat carefully crept closer sniffing as she went, butting her nose against me and Ronan until she found a spot she liked on Ronan's pillow, between his shoulder and his head. Instantly, the sound of a small motorboat filled the room, and she pushed her head against Ronan's chin.

"Is this a joke?" he asked, blowing at the cat, which did nothing.

"She's taking her guarding duties seriously," I said, choosing not to be jealous of a cat. "Don't fight it. Just sleep."

I really thought he would, but Ronan was mind over matter, and he managed to get himself out of that bed. I couldn't believe it. Neither could the cat who hissed at him. "I'm gonna take a shower," he said, and I watched him walk to the bathroom.

It was ridiculous to worry about a man like Ronan. It was like worrying over a mountain or a bullet. He didn't like it.

But I couldn't stop myself.

While he showered, with nothing else to do, I redressed in my ruined sweats, took a pain pill, and cleaned up the cottage a little. Using one hand, I stacked magazines about knitting and cooking on the edge of the table. Threw out the lettuce that was going from wilted to mushy. I opened a can of the cat's wet food, which brought her out of the bedroom to purr around my ankles. Her dark fur brushed my feet. She purred and butted her head against me full of gratitude for the bare minimum.

Just like me. God, what an embarrassing realization. Caroline had given me scraps, and I'd made a meal out of them. She'd given me lies, and I'd called it love, grateful for the chance to be manipulated.

"Poppy?" Ronan called, coming to the door dressed in fresh clothes, his hair slicked back. He rubbed a hand over his face, his beard growing in, changing the hard planes of his face. He'd never look like a teddy bear, but he did look softer. "You're all right, then?"

I stepped back from the food and the cat swept in to eat. "Tell me something; what happens to Caroline?"

"What do you mean?"

I shook my head. "Does anything ever happen to people like Caroline?"

"You want revenge?"

"I want . . . clarity. I want to know why she did what she did to me." Marrying me to the senator, killing the senator, sending Ronan into my life.

"I can tell you the answer to that," he said and came over to where I stood, vibrating with rage. He pulled me in his arms, petting me like I was the cat. "Because it served her. That's always the answer for people like Caroline. She does what she does only because it serves her. And I know you want answers and revenge, but you'll never get them from a woman like her. The ivory tower where she lives is too tall for the likes of us."

"So, I just walk away?"

"You walk away and live the best fucking life you can, Poppy. That's your revenge."

"What about you?"

He kissed me. A total distraction move. I got the message; his future wasn't something he was going to talk about. Just like his past.

This kiss tasted like tears. Like ash. Like the end. It tasted the same as the beginning.

Having emptied the bowl, the cat began curling around Ronan's ankles, purring and butting her head against him.

"What do you want, you wee beast?" he asked, picking up the cat to look in its eyes.

"Father Patrick said it was part of a feral cat colony that used to live here."

The cat hissed. Ronan hissed back and then put the cat under his arm, scratching its chin.

"All those cats were killed," Ronan said, confirming in his roundabout way he had been at this school. That he knew Father Patrick.

"Sinead saved three."

"Really?" he asked. I nodded.

The purring started again.

Ugh. We're both so shameless. Doing anything for a scratch on the head.

I looked out the kitchen window. On the hilltop, the priest was back out in his garden, pulling a roll of chicken wire out of the shed. He was going to fix the part of the fence the deer had ruined. And I could stay in this cottage with Ronan and his silence and my dead-end desire, or I could go do something useful.

"I'm going to go help Father Patrick," I said, because the decision was easy.

"What?"

"He's repairing his fence and I think he needs help."

"Poppy. You need to dye your hair."

I walked to the door and shoved my feet back in the boots. I picked up the sling and put it on.

The pain meds were already dulling my shoulder again. "You don't have to come," I said, actually wishing he wouldn't. I needed some distance. I needed to pick myself up, dust myself off, and remember there was no part of Ronan Byrne I would get to hold onto.

CHAPTER ELEVEN
Ronan

Damn her. I watched her walk up the steps to the church through the window, the wind picking up her hair and sending it streaming behind her. She wore shapeless black clothes that hid her small body, the curves and planes of which were burned onto my skin. How long, I wondered, would it take not to feel her against me, like some phantom pain?

The priest saw her coming and waved at her with his whole arm. Poppy waved back.

Damn him too.

Damn him, especially.

I wasn't helping them. That was for fucking sure. If she was fool enough to go over there with fifty stitches in her arm, that was on her.

The cat suddenly sank her claws in my arm and screeched at me, and I realized I'd been squeezing her too tight. "Sorry," I muttered and let her go. She jumped onto the chair and licked her paws, glaring at me.

On the hill, Poppy and the priest were struggling with the roll of chicken wire. She kept dropping her end because she was trying to do it one-handed.

Not that I was going to help.

I turned away from the window and the blue file folder on the mantel caught my eye.

Shoulda burned it.

It was only a matter of time before Poppy looked at it. She'd noticed it during that ridiculous conversation about names. She was foolish, but she wasn't dumb. She knew the folder was *something*.

Intending to toss it in the fire again, I grabbed the folder over the mantel. But as was the case with all my intentions here, they dissolved the second I had the thing in my hands.

I opened it.

My marks at St. Brigid's were up top. Dismal. I tried to remember the last class I'd been in where I'd cared about marks. There'd been Mrs. Daniels in first class. She'd had a nice voice and a lot of patience. After lunch, she'd read *Charlotte's Web* to us. I might have tried for her. But by the time I was sixteen, marks were no longer the point.

After my St. Brigid's marks, there was a picture of all of us, the boys of St. Brigid's in our jumpers and long pants standing in front of that whalebone altar the priests were so proud of, like they'd carved it themselves. Tom and I were standing together, glaring at the camera, matching black eyes and tough-guy expressions. God, Tom loved a fight. From the looks of us, the picture would have been about a month before everything had fallen apart.

On the far side of Tom was Father Patrick. And next to Father Patrick was Father McConal. Father Patrick looked young. Younger than I remembered him being. Like he struggled to grow facial hair. He had his head turned in the picture, looking at Tom and me.

Father McConal was looking at the camera with that smug half smile on his face, daring the world to say anything about the way he handled the school and the boys placed in his care.

"Pikey Tom had something to say about it, didn't he?" I murmured. Tommy had said it the only way he could. With the only power he felt he had left.

"Jesus," I muttered and tossed the folder on the pile of magazines Poppy had straightened up. I checked my phone for word from Glenn who made fake documents. I'd known Glenn when we were both young and coming up. I had a reputation for being fearless and he had a reputation for being meticulous.

I'd been shocked to realize he was still in operation. But when I'd left Derry for Belfast, he'd stayed behind, always content living under the radar. Which was how he never ended up in jail. Or dead. Small kingdoms, he always said, never get taken down. And clearly, he'd been right.

I could trust Glenn. He didn't know the Morellis or Caroline, and Caroline definitely didn't know him.

But now there was a plan, and a plan meant the clock was on.

There were no texts from Glenn. The world swam around me. Adrenaline came and went, and when it went, I was left even more tired than I'd been before. The room was warm, and if I sat in that chair behind me, I'd be asleep in a second. I was practically asleep on my feet.

I paced, keeping myself conscious.

On the hill, Father Patrick and Poppy were still struggling with the chicken wire.

It was only a matter of time before she . . . yep. Dropped it. The chicken wire rolled down the hill, unspooling before Poppy could grab it. With her bad arm.

The cat made a horrible screeching sound and I turned to find her at the door, scratching at the wood and yelling at me.

"You want out?" I asked. The cat yelled some more.

"There are animals out there that want to eat you, ya know? You were almost killed once, or don't you remember?"

The cat, much like Poppy, didn't seem to care. I stomped across the room to open the door and then followed the cat out.

Only because Poppy was going to hurt herself if someone didn't help. And other than the cat and a priest who'd never helped anyone, I was the only someone around.

"Hey!" Poppy called as I approached. The sea gulls were out in full force over near the side entrance to the church and I remembered, all at once and deeply against my will, that Father Patrick always fed the sea gulls. Just like he'd fed those fucking cats. "Everything all right?"

"You're going to open your stitches," I said and picked up the giant roll of chicken wire by myself. I turned on the priest who was watching me with an open mouth and barely restrained fear. "Where do you want this?"

"I, ah . . . well."

I turned to Poppy who pointed at the far corner of the garden, and I carried the wire over my shoulder down the sloping hill. The sun was hot, but the breeze was cool—a combination of perfection I'd forgotten about while living in New York, where it was either hot or cold with nothing in between. I'd missed the way the ocean smelled up here. New York City was near the very same ocean, but it never smelled like this. Deep brine and fresh.

I dropped the chicken wire on its end right near the spot where the fencing had been bent back, probably by the deer. "You have snips?" I asked, and the priest pulled them out of his pocket.

"I can handle it from here," he said. "There's no need—"

I stepped back and the roll of wire started to fall. Of course Poppy stepped forward to grab it, and I caught it and her before she got there. "Just give me the snips," I said to the priest who clearly had not gotten any better at taking care of people.

"I got it," the priest said with a hard edge to his voice. He came to stand next to me and pulled the edge of chicken wire while I unspooled it.

When he had enough, he crouched and clipped each wire one by one.

"Careful," he said as the wire popped free and caught on the edge of my sweater. Poppy untangled me.

"I like that sweater," she said with a saucy look at me under her lashes. Daft girl, flirting with me in front of a priest. I liked the shamelessness of it. Of her in the sunlight on a hilltop. In a garden.

"Do you remember this garden?" Father Patrick asked, looking up at me, a half smile on his face. Like he was reading my mind, like we were all having such a good time. "It's the same one you helped—"

"I don't remember the fucking garden," I snapped at him.

Once the wire was free, I took the roll back up the sloped hill to the shed where, in the darkness that smelled of cedar mulch and mud, I had a strange sense of déjà vu. The garden tools were all hung on a pegboard. The rakes and shovels were clean and resting against the walls next to big bags of fertilizer and mulch sitting in buckets.

We do that so the mice don't get into them.

Rattled by the memory, I got out of the shed.

"You done?" I asked when I got back to the

edge of that garden. Father Patrick was bending the edges of the wire over the existing chicken wire so it hung in the right place.

"Just about," Poppy said.

"I've expanded it over the years," Father Patrick said, like someone had asked him. "The one we built was about half this size."

"You built this garden?" Poppy asked me, bright-eyed, like I'd taught the cat to talk.

"No."

"We're going to make a garden, boys. We're going to break the ground and fertilize it. We're going to plant seeds and do everything we can to help them grow."

"Fuck all grows up here," Tommy said. Snarled, really. And I snarled with him because that was what I did. Father Patrick didn't even say anything about the language. He was disappointing that way. Refusing to be provoked when provoking the priests was what we lived for.

But truly, our hearts weren't in it.

Father Patrick had pulled us out of the punishment Father McConal had given us and we were calmed by the sunshine and fresh air. And weak from hunger.

The priest couldn't keep his mouth shut. "You built this before—"

"No," I said.

Poppy blinked at me, accepting my lie for what it was—the end of this conversation.

"After we finish here," she asked. "Do this do you think we could go help Father Patrick—?"

"No," I said.

"But there's wire over the windows in the sanctuary and it would be so pretty without it."

"Did you tell her why there's wire over the windows in the sanctuary?" I asked Father Patrick, who nodded while not looking up from the fence repair.

"Father Patrick told me that boys used to throw rocks," Poppy said.

Father Patrick sat us down with our backs to the church so anyone looking at us wouldn't see and he gave us rolls from breakfast, stuffed with ham. All the cats came out at the smell of that salty ham.

"Oh, look at you, you wee beggar," Tommy said with never-before-seen sweetness. He pulled a piece of ham off his sandwich, even though I could hear his stomach growling. Father Patrick watched Tommy, and I wanted to tell him to stop showing the priest so much weakness.

"The boy who used to throw those rocks was my friend," I said, staring at the top of Father Patrick's head. "You remember Pikey Tom, don't you, Father?" Apparently, I hadn't grown out of provoking priests.

"Of course," he said and pushed himself to his feet. He met my eyes like a man on the wrong side of a firing squad. "Do you?"

"Of course I fucking remember Tommy," I said. "What the hell kind of question is that?"

"It's been a long time and you've been gone. It's sometimes easy to forget the things that cause us pain."

Poppy was watching this all with wide eyes and I knew there'd be a litany of questions from her once we got back in the cottage. This was such a mistake. I knew it when I decided to come here.

"Why do you stay, Father?" I asked, stepping a little closer. Intimidating the smaller weaker man. At least, that was my plan, but the father only watched me. Tougher than he'd been when we'd met. When we'd built this garden.

"It's my home," he said.

"It's a shit home."

He nodded, accepting the idea. "I understand how you might think that."

"Come on, Poppy," I said. "Let's go back to the cottage."

"No. I want to help take down the chain

link."

"I have to go into the village, lass," Father Patrick said with a smile that made me crazy. It was so kind and understanding. Benevolent. The same way he looked at Tommy when he asked if he could help feed those stupid cats. "The chain link will wait."

"We won't be here much longer," she said. "This is kind of your last chance for help taking it down."

"Then I suppose it can stay up," he said, and I wanted to punch that smile right off his face. "There are worse things."

I took Poppy's hand, eager to get her away from that smile. That shed. That garden. All the worse things.

"Ronan," he said, and Poppy stopped, all but forcing me to turn around.

"What?"

"There is something you could do for me."

That I managed not to laugh in his face was a real win for me.

"Consider forgiveness," he said, and at that, I could not control myself. I stepped back up the hill to him. Close enough to knock him to the ground if it came to that. Poppy came with me, holding onto my arm like she had a chance in hell of stopping me.

"For you? Never."

"Forgiveness is not for the one being forgiven," he said. Calmly, patiently, like I was still that kid with the temper. With the black eyes. With that friend who was still alive. "It's for the one who forgives. Shed this darkness, son."

"I'm not your goddamned son!"

He talked over me like I'd never said a word. "Shed this darkness before it's the only thing you have left. Tommy wouldn't want—"

"You don't know what Tommy would want!" I snapped at the man. "Tommy would want to be alive. He'd want to be kicking your ass when you dropped off that file. He'd want a wife and kids and whole goddamned life that you took from him."

"I know," the priest said in the way of the resigned. "I know."

"Ronan?" Poppy whispered, her hand covering my fist. "Let's go. Take me back to the cottage."

She pulled me out of that rage, that darkness and memory, and led me by the hand back to the cottage. The cat met us at the door, screeching at us like we'd missed curfew. Poppy opened the door, and we all went inside. She didn't say anything. She didn't try to touch me. Or hug me. She stepped away from me and just watched.

"Who was Tommy?"

"A friend."

"At the school?"

I nodded, my lips closed, trying to keep the story down as best I could, though it seemed to want to be told.

"What happened to him?"

"The priests killed him."

"Literally?" she asked, unable to hide her shock.

"They killed all the damn cats," he said. "And they might as well have killed him too."

"What can I do for you?"

I thought of the millions of cruel and hurtful things I could say to her that would slice me open and spill some of the bile in the back of my throat.

But she didn't deserve that.

And there was nowhere to go. Nothing to do. I could lay her out on the floor in front of the fire. I could touch her until she was the only thing that mattered. I could distract myself from my pain with her pleasure.

But she didn't deserve that either.

She didn't deserve a single thing that had

happened to her. Least of all me.

"I'm going to take a shower," I said.

I stayed in the shower until the hot water ran out and then I stayed in a little longer until the cold water didn't hurt anymore. When I was numb, I turned off the water and wrapped myself in another of Sinead's flowered towels. She had a real "woman on my own" aesthetic. I opened the bathroom door only to find Poppy just outside it.

Asleep.

Her body against the wall, her head tilted uncomfortably to the side. Her legs stretched out in front of her. Asleep against the wall when the bed was right there. The daft girl. But then I realized being uncomfortable had been the point. She'd been trying to stay awake.

What would it be like? I wondered. What would it be like to deserve her? To have her be mine? What kind of fortune would that be? The kind I couldn't even imagine; I lacked the creativity. The understanding of that kind of luck.

Carefully, so I didn't wake her and I didn't hurt her arm, which she'd been abusing up in that garden, I picked her up. At the movement, my blue file folder slipped out from behind her.

Jesus Christ. It was too much to hope she had respected my privacy and not looked.

Well, half of it she already knew. The rest of it she had to be able to guess. How strange to have so many secrets known by someone else.

I set her back down in the bed. On the side table were her meds. After her work in the garden, she must have taken one for pain and that was why she was asleep.

The sooner I got her away from this place and to her sister, the better. The rest of her life was waiting for her. Even as part of me wanted to keep her here. Just a bit longer. A few hours. A day.

This time when the knock on the door came, it was a surprise, a sign I was getting too comfortable. Soft. The gun I'd left on the mantel slipped into my hand like it had been born there and again, I used the barrel to lift the edge of the curtain.

It was Father Patrick. Again. Looking furtively around him like bad guys lurked in the shadows.

Jesus. This fucking guy.

"Yeah?" I asked when I opened the door.

"I got an answer from Poppy's sister's number."

Right. The words hit me like bullets. The world was in motion and I couldn't pretend for another minute that she wasn't in danger. I could have her or she could be safe.

There couldn't be both.

"What did it say?"

"Just asked which village?"

"Did you answer?"

"No, look—" The father held out his phone and I grabbed it.

Which village? was in the last text bubble. And I didn't know Zilla at all, but that didn't sound like any loving sister I knew. I opened the phone, pulled out the sim card, and crushed it with my foot.

I'd been a fool. Hoping for the best when I knew that was a sucker's game. I had a window, a tiny impossible window, to get Poppy new documents and a new life. And I'd been in this cottage playing pretend.

"What are you doing?" Father Patrick asked.

"Is there any place you can go for a few days?" I asked him.

"Go? No. This is my home."

"It would be safer for you if you left for a little bit."

"What about Sinead?'

"Sinead's safe; I'm asking about you?"

"I'm not leaving the church, Ronan. I'm safe there."

"The Heavenly Father isn't going to protect you from the people who are coming this way, Father. They'll kill you in a church as easily as they'd kill you any place else."

"All the same," he said. "What will you be doing?"

"The less you know, the better."

"But Poppy . . . she'll be all right, won't she?'

"Yes," I said. I'd make sure of it as it would probably be the last thing I'd do. "Go home, Father—"

I went to close the door and the father put his hand out. "I'll pray for you, Ronan."

"Pray for Poppy, Father Patrick. There's no saving me."

CHAPTER TWELVE

POPPY

THE NEXT MORNING, there was a strange woman in the kitchen. In the kitchen I—in a very short period of time—had come to think of as our kitchen. Mine and Ronan's.

She was short with a pile of graying red hair on top of her head, and she was humming off tune as she put wet food in the cat's bowl. The cat was trying to climb up her leg, her purr audible from across the room.

"Hello?" I called, my voice croaky from sleep.

She whirled, a hand pressed to her chest. "Jaysusmaryandjoseph," she said, her accent so thick, it took me a second to understand her words. "Gave me a fright, you did." She gathered herself and smiled at me in such a way that all I could do was smile back. "Well, you look like you had a bad dose. How are you feeling?"

"Fine," I said. "Good. I'm sorry . . . I don't remember your name."

"Well, I'm guessing so. You were pretty knackered when we met. I'm Sinead. This is my gaff."

I guessed from the way she was gesturing around her that she meant the house was hers. "Well, thank you so much for letting us stay here."

"Well, there's no saying no to Ronan, is there?"

I felt a blush incinerate my face. "No," I said. "Not really. I'm Poppy."

"Well, it's real nice to meet you. Formal, like."

The cat sounded like a motor in the room. "What's the cat's name?"

"Rascal. I see you've been feeding her. I was going to take her with me, but the old broad doesn't take to change and there's too much chaos at my daughter's place. I thought she'd sneak out the door here first chance she got and head up to Father Patrick. He's known to leave her a bit of cream now and again."

"He's very nice," I said.

"He's not so bad."

"Your cat is nice too."

"No, she's not," Sinead said, giving the cat a scratch behind the ears, which made Rascal hiss.

We both laughed a little.

"How . . . ah . . . how do you know Ronan?" I had this weird half idea that she might be Ronan's family. An aunt of some kind? But I couldn't actually imagine him having this warm person in his life and still being quite so feral.

"Oh," she said with a wince. "That's his story to tell. Not mine."

A lot of that going around.

"Sure," I said, falling back on old habits. "I'm sorry to pry."

"You hungry, like? I've got—"

"Coffee?"

She smiled and turned to pour me a cup from Ronan's French press.

"Where is Ronan?" I asked.

"Out on the wee wall over there," she said, pointing behind her like I could see through the stone walls. "He wanted you to do this when you got up."

She set the box of hair dye on the counter. Right. I'd forgotten. I flipped the color over and read the name. "Dark Chocolate."

"Yeah." Sinead looked about as sold on the idea as I felt.

"Thank you," I said and took the box only to set it on the table behind me. She handed me a cup of coffee and I smiled at her. "I'm just gonna go have a chat with Ronan."

Sinead's merry laugh followed me out into the bright sunshine of the day. The air felt warmer, like the sun was just a bit hotter today than the other day. The wind, for the moment, was at rest.

Ronan sat on the hip-high stone wall. He was a black slice out of the green and blue of the land and sky behind him. I watched as he drank his coffee and stared out at the ocean as it made its way toward the rocks beneath us.

"Good morning," I said as I got close enough to him.

He wore a pair of dark sunglasses that only added to the mystery and appeal of him, and all my body could do was remember, with one full-body shiver, what this man could do to me. How the other night I slept with his come on my skin and his scent in my nose and seven million questions about him rattling around in my brain.

"You haven't dyed your hair," he said by way of greeting. I couldn't tell with him in those sunglasses if he were looking at me or not, so I pulled myself back into my shell, or whatever shell he allowed me to have around him.

"I just woke up. Are we in some kind of rush?"

"Father Patrick heard back from your sister's number last night."

"Zilla!"

"I don't think it was your sister texting."

"Someone else has her phone?"

He nodded.

"Someone bad?"

Again, he nodded.

"Oh." That was all I could say. "What do we do?"

"The fake paperwork is going to be ready for you tomorrow morning. My contact needs a picture emailed to him straight away."

"That's why you want me to dye my hair."

"The priest didn't say what village we were in. Only that we were outside of Carrickfergus, which narrows things down. Even more if they were able to track where the message came from. As soon as your paperwork is ready, we're leaving."

I felt his fear more profoundly than I felt my own and it was strange, but instead of making me more scared, all it did was make me feel such worry for him. Braving an inevitable rejection, I stepped in front of him, and, to my surprise, he didn't jerk away. I shifted forward between his knees and he let me. He let me put my hand against his face, stroking the scar along his jaw. I held my breath, waiting for him to bare his teeth.

But he only sighed. Deeply. Heavily. And rested his face in my hands.

"Have you slept?"

"It's been a busy night."

"Ronan—"

"I thought we'd have more time," he whispered. And it was only because he was so tired that he would say that. Reveal that. He was exhausted and there was a clock ticking in his head. But still, his words wrapped around me. A comfort he wouldn't like giving me, but I took all the same.

"How about you take a nap and I'll dye my hair."

He reached up and pulled on a blond curl hanging over my shoulder. "I wish I could see it red. The way it's supposed to be."

"Maybe you will," I said, trying to sound both reassuring and flirtatious.

"No. I won't." And then he stood, his hands on my face, and kissed me. Kissed me like it was a battle he needed to win, and I could not surrender fast enough. He was heavy against me, and I knew this kiss was something he'd regret later.

I was tired of regrets.

"Come on," I said, leading him off the wall

and toward the cottage.

Sinead was putting on her coat when we walked in. "I brought you some more food," she said. "Put clean sheets on the bed. I'll be back—"

"We will be gone tomorrow," I said.

"Oh," Sinead went still. "That's good, I suppose."

"You'll want to stay away a few more days," Ronan said, and he pulled out a stack of bills from his wallet. I could see American dollars, British pounds, and even euros. He could bribe his way across Europe if he had to. "Just to be safe."

"Are you safe?" Sinead asked quietly, like she didn't want me to hear her.

"As safe as I've ever been." Which was his way of saying—not much at all.

Sinead pursed her lips at him and then she was gone. Starting up her old car and driving down the dirt road toward town. Ronan scrubbed at his face, pushed his hands in his hair, looked for all the world like a man at the end of his rope.

"You need to dye your hair, Poppy, so we can take a picture and send it." He reached for more coffee, but I put my hand on his arm, stopping him.

"And you need to get some sleep, or you'll be no good to anyone."

He didn't argue with me but turned to the chair, where he'd been sleeping what little he slept in the three nights we'd been here. "No," I urged. "Go to the bedroom. The sheets are clean." He looked like he might fight me, but I started to push him toward the bedroom. He didn't fight me, which told me just how exhausted he was.

"You're no good to anyone like this. Least of all me. And I'm expecting you to keep me safe."

"Are ya?"

"I am. So you need at least an hour's sleep. I'll hold down the fort."

"And dye your hair."

"All of it. I'll do all of it. You just get some rest."

He sat on the side of the bed and picked up the blue file folder I'd found last night from the bedside table. It was burnt a little, so I'd seen that picture of him as a kid. He'd been arrested for stealing a car, which must have been what sent him to St. Brigid's.

"Did you read this?" he asked.

I shook my head. "Only the first page. When I realized what it was, I shut it. I was going to talk to you about it, but I fell asleep."

"Not much to talk about." He held the folder in his hand like he was weighing it.

"It's . . . it's your whole life, Ronan. How can you say that?"

"Because I haven't had much of a life."

"That's not true," I whispered.

"I've been a criminal and killer. I've been a tool used by rich people to keep their rich world in order. I've—"

"You saved my life."

"That might be the one good thing I've done."

He thinks he's going to die. Because of me.

My stomach rolled over, sick and slimy.

"You still have a lot of life left," I told him. "There's a chance for you to change things."

He looked at me, his eyes dark with exhaustion and resignation. And pity for me, like my hope was just ridiculous. "Monsters like me don't get a happy ending, Poppy."

I touched his face, his shoulder. But he was cold and still and a million miles away.

"You're not a monster, Ronan. You're not—"

"My birth certificate's in there." He interrupted me like the subject of his being a monster was closed.

"Did you look?" I remembered he didn't know his mother. Or where he'd been born. "You should look. Let's look."

"Doesn't change anything," he said and tossed the file down on the side of the bed. Finally, he lay down, his eyes shut. Like he just couldn't fight it anymore. Sleep and everything that followed were inevitable.

I wanted to weep and scream and do anything to change his mind. To convince him he mattered. That I would fight for him if he would let me. I sat there trembling, and he rolled over onto his side. His back to me.

"Wake me up in an hour," he said. I waited until he was asleep and then picked up the file and put it back in the other room. He might not care right now, but that wasn't going to be true forever. There might come a time when he'd want to know the circumstances of his birth.

Because this wasn't the end of him. *I will not be the end of him.*

CHAPTER THIRTEEN

ZILLA USED TO change her hair color all the time. Her red was browner than mine, and she'd dyed it purple and pink. She'd shave half her head at a time. I'd left mine long and curly, only dying it blond when the senator informed me I didn't have a choice about it.

I didn't have a choice about this, either, I guessed. But it felt different. Truthfully, everything felt different. In the bathroom, I stripped to my waist, squeezed all the chemicals onto my hair, and piled the tresses up on my head. In the cabinet under the sink, I found some bright pink fingernail polish and decided to paint my toes while I had the time to kill, all while coming to grips with the reality I was about to enter a brand-new life.

While Ronan thought this was the end of his.

I wished with everything I had in me that we could just stop. Stop time. Stay in this cottage for another day. Year.

To what end? a voice in my head that sounded

remarkably like my sister asked. *Monsters are fun to fuck, but dangerous to love.*

And didn't I have enough danger?

Sure. More than enough. More than enough for three lifetimes, but it didn't seem right that I was going to dye my hair, change my name, and go off and have a life while Ronan was going to . . . what?

Die?

And I just had to be okay with it? Already the pain of saying goodbye to him was something I was putting away. Shoving aside the way Ronan himself had taught me.

When the time was up and my nails were dry, I stepped into the shower and rinsed out my hair, dark brown rivers of water running over my breasts and stomach and down between my legs to pool at my feet. I wiggled my bright pink toes in the suds.

We had twenty-four hours, and that was something. Twenty-four hours to change his mind about going back. He didn't have to come with me, but why did he have to go back to Bishop's Landing? To the Constantines? To that monster life no man should have?

One day had never seemed so short.

My hair was soft and a little limp from the

treatment and ... very brown. Black-brown, even. Far edgier against my pale skin than anything I'd ever had before, which made its length look all wrong. Punk Stepford wife wasn't a good look for anyone, and so I did what I'd never done before.

Cut my own hair.

A ponytail and a sharp pair of scissors got rid of most of the length and after that, it was just a matter of cutting into the hair vertically, making pieces and edges where there weren't any. And after toweling it dry and adding a dollop of ancient mousse I'd found in the bathroom cabinet, I had to admit it looked like shit, but I didn't look at all like myself.

And that was the point.

I opened the door to the bathroom, expecting Ronan to be sound asleep. Only to find him awake. And pointing a gun at me. Which should've made my heart stop. Just something else to add to the list of things I was used to.

"Fuck." He shook off the sleep and put the gun back down on the bedside table. "Sorry."

"It's not the first time you've pointed a gun at me, is it?"

He looked at me sideways and then reluctantly smiled. "Your hair," he said. "Ya cut it."

"Yeah. I thought maybe it would help."

"You look so different, Poppy," he said with some wonder.

"Truthfully, I feel different." I put my hands on my hips. "How are you going to take this picture?"

He pulled his new cheap cell phone out of his back pocket.

"I need one of those," I said.

"We'll pick it up when we get your new passport tomorrow. Now . . ." He took me by the shoulders and positioned me up against a white wall. "That should work. Don't smile."

For some reason, that made me smile, and he shot me an exasperated look.

"Am I Beth in this new passport?

"Yep."

"Where am I from?"

"Brussels. An EU passport gives you a few more options for hiding out."

"I'm Belgian. That's fun."

"I honestly don't know anyone on the run who has been so okay with it."

"Remember what you said when we met?" I asked. "It all depends on what's coming through your door . . ."

It felt like a lifetime ago when he'd said that

to me. The girl in the dress didn't even seem like me, that was how much I felt like I'd changed since then.

"Aye," he said. "I remember. Come on, let's do this picture."

"I'm going to try very hard to look Belgian." He shook his head, but I could tell he was smiling at me.

✧ ✧ ✧

Ronan

"Now what?" she asked after I'd sent the picture. I knew what she was angling at, but someone had to keep their wits about them.

"Why aren't you scared?" I asked, because she stood there with her terrible haircut and two families after her, the rest of her life buried in the unknown, and she was smiling at me.

"You won't let anything happen to me."

"You don't seem to understand that I'm the thing that happened to you."

She took a deep breath, like she was thinking it over. "I guess I don't see it that way. Can I ask you a question?"

"I'm pretty sure I can't stop you."

"Why are you going back?"

"To get answers."

"I don't care about the answers."

"Someone wants you dead or alive, Poppy, and you don't care?"

"Not if you're going to get hurt."

Oh. This. I'd thought we could skip this part.

"I'm not going with you, Poppy."

"I'm not asking you to. I'm just asking you not to go back there." She stepped forward and I stepped back. And then gave up the dance altogether and went around her into the living room. God, this fucking place was so small.

"Ronan." She followed. Of course she followed. She was a goddamned dog with a bone, and I needed to smack her to get her to drop it. I just... I didn't have the will to smack her anymore. She didn't deserve my cruelty.

"If I don't go back," I said, "you'll be hiding forever. You'll never have your money. You'll never have your name—"

"I don't care about those things."

"What about your sister?"

"Trust me, she doesn't care. Ronan—"

She reached for me, the edjit, her hand closing around mine. "Go anywhere but back," she said. "You don't have to tell me where you go. I won't follow you like some lovesick girl. I just can't stand the idea of you going back and getting hurt because of me."

"It's not just because of you," he said. "I have my own reckoning with Caroline. My own questions I need answered. For me, Poppy. Nothing to do with you."

"What can I say that will change your mind?"

"Nothing. Not one thing, Poppy. It's done."

She took a deep breath that shuddered at the top and then when she let it go. Her eyes were on the ceiling, and I could see her blinking back tears. "I don't want to spend the last of our time fighting. And I really don't want to spend it crying."

When she finally looked at me, the invitation was in her eyes. Her face. It was clear how she'd spend the last of our time and my dick went hard at the thought.

I pulled my hand free and stepped back.

She sighed, disappointed. "I feel like I've been begging for you to touch me since the moment we met. And . . . I'm done doing that. We've got another few hours to spend here, and I can read a fucking book or we can make each other feel good. But it's your decision. I'm done feeling like I'm forcing your hand just by asking for what I want."

She stared at me a second longer and my

silence—my inaction—disappointed her more. "I'm going to build up the fire." She walked around me to the fireplace. Behind me, I heard her fumbling for a second and then the crackle of kindling. I could even hear her blowing on the wood, encouraging it to catch.

You're a selfish prick. My father's voice in my head was scathing. *Ya always were. Only looking out for yourself. You'd fuck that girl into next week and never think twice.*

But I always thought twice. Always. And this was a moment that wouldn't come again. It made me feral. Wild.

I could hurt her.

She would like it.

The thought of her pleasure at the edge of my violence made it inevitable. I wanted to hurt her and be hurt by her. I wanted to drown in the pleasure and the pain we'd give each other.

And then I wanted to walk away and seal this part of myself, this weak and vulnerable part of myself, up like a brick wall so I never fucking felt this way again.

"Poppy." That was all I said. Her name. But it was full of my intentions toward her. My wicked depraved intentions.

She stood to face me, breathing deep. Her

nipples beneath the borrowed shirt she wore were hard, and if I got my hands inside those sweatpants, I'd find her drenched. For me. For this.

I could smell it in the air.

"You don't scare me," she whispered, though a little bit of her was lying.

"I should."

"You're going to give me some big speech about how you're going to hurt—"

I cut her off with my fist in her hair. She gasped, going up on her toes. My desire was a tidal wave. An onslaught. "Say stop and I'll stop."

Her eyes went wide as if she was just understanding what she'd signed up for at this moment. And then I kissed her, open mouthed, my hands in her hair, holding her still. I plundered her. I sucked and bit and she let me. She bit back. Her tongue was in my mouth and her hands were around my waist, tangled in my shirt, holding onto me.

"Stop," she panted, and I stopped. My mouth a breath away from hers. The only things moving were my heart pounding my chest and my blood filling my cock.

She licked her lips. "Just checking." She grinned at me and I pulled her up and against me, refusing to laugh. Refusing to admire her. To fucking like her.

I rubbed my thumb over her lips, prying my way inside. Not that she refused me. Not that she had one single defense. "Suck," I whispered, looking into her eyes, daring her to look away. But she didn't. She looked right back at me and sucked on my thumb. Biting it with her teeth. "I've got twelve hours to fuck you until I don't give a shit about you."

She jerked back, shaking her head. "It doesn't work that way."

Silent, I stepped back until the backs of my legs hit the chair. I put my hands on her shoulders and pushed her down on her knees. Her hands settled on my thighs. Her lips curled into a smile that was going to be the death of me.

"I know you," she said. "And I know how you like to play."

"You think this is a game?" I asked and she nodded. I sat down in the chair with her kneeling between my legs. "Undo my pants."

CHAPTER FOURTEEN

Ronan

THE WORDS WERE barely out of my mouth before her shaking, cool fingers wiggled under the edge of my shirt, undoing the buttons of the jeans and lowering the zipper. I shifted, letting her pull the pants down so my cock sprang free.

She glanced up at me and I saw her nerves. I saw her sweetness. And the selfish asshole in me wanted to keep it. Have it. I wanted all that sweetness to be mine forever. And fuck, she thought she wanted that too. She thought I was worth saving. Worth giving herself to, and that was a temptation I never thought I'd have to battle before. But I knew who I was, and I knew what her life should look like. It didn't include the likes of me.

"Can I . . . I mean, do you want . . . ?"

"Your mouth on me? Yeah, I want your fucking mouth."

The touch of her lips blew my head off. She ruined me in a breath. In a touch. Her soft hand wrapped around my cock and her mouth slipped over the head and her tenderness was all wrong.

I put my hand over hers, tightening her fist around me until the pleasure was part pain. She watched me with her dark eyes and then smiled at me.

"I like it that way too," she whispered. Hard, she meant. Rough, she meant. Like I didn't know how she liked her pleasure. And I was glad she had the nerve to say it because maybe she'd say it to the next guy and they'd have a shot—

Fuck. No.

I went blind with rage. With a territorial instinct I could not control. The thought of any other man getting to see her on her knees in front of them was unacceptable. As much as it was undeniable.

Mine.

She reached between my legs, her nails scraping across the sensitive skin of my balls and the inside of my thighs. She reached up under my sweater for the naked skin of my chest. She ran those nails across my nipples. Hard enough to hurt.

My laughter was a dark growl in my throat,

the animal in me taking over. I wrapped my fingers in her hair, clenching my fist. She gasped, tilting her head back, her throat such a beautiful fragile arch.

And her smile. Her fucking smile. I'd go to my grave thinking about that smile. Knowing and innocent all at once. She was every dichotomy, endlessly fascinating.

It took no urging for her to bend over me, her mouth closing over the tip of my cock.

"More," I told her. "Take more."

And she did. Slick and hot, she took more of my cock. I waited for her to stop, to pull back, but she didn't, and my hands in her hair holding on. Holding tight.

"Yes," I breathed, half out of my mind with lust and pride. "Like that. Take it all the . . ." I arched into her, electricity running through me as she swallowed me deep. I bit my lip against everything I wanted to say. About how beautiful she was. How perfect. I swallowed all those words back down to where they came from.

Poppy hummed in her throat, the vibrations a special new torture. I held her head with both hands and fucked myself up into her as hard and high as I could go. Again. And then again.

And still, she surrendered.

What else would she give me? What more could I take from her? The thought of easing my cock deep into her asshole sent me hard over the edge and my orgasm nearly broke me in two.

"Jesus . . . fuck, Poppy."

I let go of her, not wanting to hurt her, and she stayed with me to the end. Curled over me, milked everything out of me, until finally, with a gasp, she fell back on her heels. Her eyes streaming. Her lips red.

Smiling.

"That was . . ."

I couldn't let her finish. A sudden and primal survival instinct lifted out of my childhood maybe. I didn't fucking know. All I knew was the only way to survive this . . . us . . . was to not put anything into words. That way, years from now, I could convince myself this girl and the way she'd made me feel had been a fever dream. The effect of too little sleep.

Careful of her shoulder I lifted her into my lap, arranging her around me so I could kiss her as deep and as hard as I could. Kiss her like I wished I could fuck her. Completely.

I tasted myself on her, the salt and tang of my come, and the strange taboo of that was gone. And somewhere back in my brain, I realized the question wasn't what else would she give me, but what would I give her? What lines would I cross? What bridges would I blow up for her?

This ground we were on was too goddamned dangerous. I'd tipped us—she'd tipped me—into a mine field.

She pulled back, panting for air, and I realized I was doing the same. Both of us breathing like we were being chased.

"That," she began, insisting on smiling at me. Her shirt, the hand-me-down from Sinead, was a threadbare flannel shirt with buttons down the front. "Was amazing. You're so fucking hot, Ronan. But I was pretty amazing. That had to be the best blowjob—"

I tore open the shirt she wore. Buttons flew into the fireplace and across the room into the kitchen. Instinctively, she lifted her hands to cover herself. "You startled me!" she said with a self-deprecating laugh.

"I didn't mean to." I pulled the shirt off her shoulders. God, her breasts. Her creamy skin with the sprinkling of freckles leftover from some long-ago sunburn. There was a mole just at the edge of her ribcage.

She's just a lass who doesn't realize she deserves better than you, you cunt. My father would never say that. But his voice had become the tool I used to torture myself with the truth.

"I meant to scare you," I said and took the edges of the shirt, still buttoned at her wrists, and pulled, forcing her arms behind her back. "Does that hurt your shoulder?"

"No."

"Good." And there I tied the shirt in a knot.

She gasped, the skin of her neck turning red.

She tested the knot but couldn't move. Her breasts lifted and fell with hard breaths, thrust forward by the position of her arms. Like she was offering herself to me. Fuck, I liked that.

And so did her, judging by the way she rocked against me. I could feel her—hot and wet—through the thin cotton pants she wore. She rocked again. And again. My cock sprang hard again in a heartbeat. I did nothing, my hands on the long arms of the chair we sat in while she worked to find the friction she needed. She spread her legs out wider, trying to press harder against my cock, but the chair was too narrow. Deep as fuck, but too narrow.

She made a sound of frustration.

"What's wrong, princess?" I whispered.

"I can't . . . I need." She bent forward, and I put my arms on her elbows, pushing her back up so I could see her face. I wanted every second of this. "Help me, Ronan."

I lifted her as I stood and she sighed, pressing against my body. Her head on my shoulder. I held her like that for a second, soaking it in before I set her down on her feet and took the pants off her. I crouched, letting her rest against me as she stepped out of the legs, and then she stood naked in the bright sunlight through the kitchen windows. The sun had moved across the sky since I'd woken up from that nap.

The day, this day—our day—vanishing. Second by second.

Without warning, I put my hand over her pussy and her legs buckled, sending her falling against me. I pressed the heel of my hand down over her clit, and she arched into me. My girl wanted pressure. And I wanted to watch her come.

"Here," I murmured, stepping away and leading back to the chair. "Over the arm."

She looked at me like I wasn't making sense, and I simply lifted and shifted her until she was straddling one of the long thick arms of the chair. Her hands behind her back and the round curve of her ass were so fucking beautiful. I pushed on her back until she was leaning forward, her body against the back of the chair, and I smiled when I heard her gasp.

Her legs shifted back and widened, and I could see the clenched muscle of her asshole. She arched into the chair, grinding her pussy against the arm of that chair. I slid my hands from her shoulders down the narrow-fluted curve of her waist to her ass, palming it in both hands. Pushing her and pulling her against the chair.

"Is this . . ." She groaned. "What you want?"

Hardly. Not even a little. But it was what I could have.

"Ronan," she sobbed. Her head pressed against the chair, the muscles in her body starting to tremble and shake. "I want you inside of me. I want—"

I smacked her ass, shutting her up. These were the things we couldn't say. My handprint was pink against her creamy skin. She stilled for a second, as if processing how she felt about it. But I knew. I knew this wicked girl's heart.

"Don't," she whispered, her body back in motion. "Don't stop."

She got another smack on the ass for that, and her breath started to hitch. Her hands in fists behind her were opening and closing like she needed something to hold onto. And because I couldn't resist and because I knew she would love it, I carefully pushed my thumb against the clench of her asshole.

"What . . . what are you doing?" she asked.

"Let me in." I leaned forward, whispering it against her hair. I was close enough that her fingers brushed my cock and I hissed, so close to coming. Her touch was nearly too much.

"How?" she whimpered. "Please. I'm so . . ."

"Relax, princess. Just . . . relax."

My thumb slipped inside of her and she made a high keening sound. Her body's pulses against the chair became fast. Awkward. Sweat tricked down the sweet valley of her spine, and her hands so close to my body were more temptation than I could resist. I moved forward, curling her fingers around me.

We found a rhythm that I could have lived off of, but the end came fast. We'd burned too hot for too long, and that seemed poetic on our last day. Seemed right.

I felt her coming first, those beautiful contractions inside of her body. The trembling gaining power and conviction. I let go of my control, coming in hot spurts against her ass. A roar and a scream filled the air and it was both of us together. Loud and primal and full of madness.

Finally, she was limp against me. Against the chair. I stepped back. Untied the shirt. Watched her shake out her arms as I helped her to her feet. Her cheeks were flushed, and she winced slightly as she moved. I felt the bite of regret and responsibility and the slow poison of inevitability.

I was only ever going to hurt her.

"You all right?" I whispered.

"I don't . . ." She shook her head, so befuddled and lost and sex drunk that I was instantly awash in tenderness for her. I lifted her in my arms, and she didn't fight. She only curled up against me, trusting me against all better instincts.

I pushed open the bedroom door wider with my foot and set her on the bed with the still rumpled blankets.

"Where are you going?" she whispered as I straightened.

"Be right back," I whispered back.

In the bathroom, I washed my hands and gave myself a stern look in the mirror.

Don't be a fucking edjit, boyo, and my father told me. And he would know.

I brought back a warm washcloth and wiped her face and her neck where sweat had pooled. She turned her face into the cloth and my hand and sighed with a bone-deep pleasure.

"That was really good," she said. I tossed the washcloth on the floor in the corner and kept my silence. "Wasn't it?"

"Yeah, princess," I told her. "We fuck pretty well."

"But we don't actually fuck." I went to stand, but she grabbed my hand. "Why don't you have sex with me? Is it me? Am I doing something wrong?"

I could have thrown off her hand. I could have said something cruel and withering—*yes, it's you and your innocence and your fucking wide eyes and the lie that you think is me*—and maybe that would have been the best call. But I didn't do any of that.

I sat back down and pulled the covers up to her neck, keeping her hands underneath so she couldn't touch me. "You were a virgin on your wedding night." It wasn't a question and her face above the blankets went as white as the sheets.

"So?"

"It was part of the reason he wanted you," I said. "A girl your age who looked like you and still a virgin—you don't grow on trees."

"Why are we talking about him?" she asked, trembling and angry.

"All you've known from sex is the senator's

rape and my . . . fucking filth."

"I like your filth."

"You and me, Poppy. We weren't right from the start and you're going to have a normal life, away from the senator and away from me. You'll marry some good guy—"

"I'm never getting married again."

Her venom surprised me, and I looked down at her. "You don't know that."

"Don't I?" She was stone cold in my arms. Absolutely resolute. "No one has that much control over me again. No one requires me to sacrifice and compromise until there's nothing left of the person I am."

"I don't think all marriages are like what you had with the senator."

"Right. You have such an understanding of marriage?"

It was a direct hit and a vicious one. She was changing right under my eyes; the sweet girl was gone, replaced by this fierce woman.

"You're not any better than the senator, thinking you know what's best for me and making decisions like my opinion doesn't matter," she said. "So, you're right. I am going to go have a different life far away from you and I'm going to find a man. A good man. Who is decent and kind and who says nice things to me and thinks I'm wonderful and I'm going to let him fuck me so hard and so often—"

I put my hand over her mouth and she tried to bite me.

I think you're wonderful. I think you're the most amazing thing I've ever seen and that you let me put my blood-soaked hands on your beautiful skin is more than I can take.

"Stop," I said as she tried to kick at me with her legs.

"Get the fuck off me," she yelled through my fingers.

"I will. When you stop."

Finally, she held herself still, but I could feel the shake in her muscles. Anger and patience. She wasn't done fighting; she was just waiting for her chance.

Good girl. That's how it's done.

I didn't know why I said what I did next, maybe because I'd had two brain-rocking orgasms on no sleep, but I opened my mouth and the truth I rarely ever acknowledged in my head came out.

"My da never talked about my ma." That trembling in her went still. "Not a word. I asked once, and he said that she died giving birth. Some kind of aneurysm or blood clot. I was a kid, and I didn't understand. But it was real clear he'd loved her about as much as he loved me—which was not much. And where I grew up, boys were getting girls pregnant all the fucking time. I don't know if it was the church's fault trying to teach abstinence to a bunch of horny teenagers, or that we were broke and bored, but it was as if no one had ever heard of a condom, like. And some of the boys married the girls and they did it looking like my da, you know. Angry at the wedding. Just a shite way to start a life. To raise a family. And I imagined my poor ma was a girl like that. Saddled to some fucker who took advantage or worse because my da was that type, you know. The type to force the issue. And then she died having me. And that was the end of her story. I didn't know her, but she sure as feck deserved more than that."

Somehow, Poppy got a hand up from under the blankets and touched my face. I flinched away and she stopped.

"I'll die a bad death, princess. There's no question. Men like me, tools like me, we have short expiration dates. So, I don't have sex without protection. Because my bloodline doesn't need to be carried on. And no woman should be made to make a painful choice about having a baby she might not want because I didn't protect her. It's the rule I don't break. Not ever. And I broke a lot of rules with you, but I made sure I never had protection around you. Because you deserve better than being fucked by me."

I took a deep breath and finally met her eyes, braced for pity, but it wasn't there. I lifted my hand off her mouth and she licked her lips, leaving them shiny.

"I had two miscarriages," she said.

"I know," I said quietly. "I'm so sorry."

"The first one everyone knew about. The senator put out a fucking press release and I . . . God, I just wanted to die. When I found out I was pregnant the second time with the senator's baby," she paused, shaking her head. "I can't tell you the despair I felt. The idea of bringing a child into that house. With that man. I mean . . . with my first pregnancy, I was hopeful. I thought I could love a baby enough to shield it from the senator. To negate whatever awful things he might do—"

"My ma probably thought the same thing," I said, and then because we were on some kind of raft floating adrift of our lives and none of this really mattered, I crawled up into the bed beside her. My arm around her, her soft weight against me.

"But the second time, I was so scared. And . . . God, I've never talked about this." She looked up at the ceiling, blinking back tears. I pulled her tighter. Held her closer.

"I don't remember, like, *planning* it," she said. "But I just . . . I did everything I could to make him mad."

I sucked in a breath when it struck me what she was saying.

"And it's not like it was hard. Everything made him mad. Everything was a reason to punish me. And so, I just did it. I didn't answer him when he talked to me. I walked into his office without asking permission. I didn't plan or make dinner. I stayed in bed until he was already up. I left my makeup all over the bathroom. In one day, I did everything I'd ever been taught not to do in front of the senator."

"So he'd hit you?"

"So he'd *beat* me. Just knock the shit out of me. And he did. And I miscarried." She looked at me stone cold, a woman at peace with the choices she'd made when every single option was awful. "He had this doctor who would come to the house and wouldn't say anything when he saw the truth of how our lives were. And when the doctor told him I was miscarrying? The way he looked at me... he knew. He knew I'd done it all on purpose."

Her whole body shook.

"The crazy thing was that I'd expected to die. I thought for sure he would kill me and I... was ready for that."

I turned on my side and shifted her so her back was all against the front of me. We breathed in unison. Our hearts beat at the same pace. I felt the tension in her melt away, bit by bit, and the warm drip of tears against my hand where it held her close.

"Survival is ugly," I said. "But surviving is a thing of beauty. You are a thing of beauty, Poppy. The most beautiful thing I've ever seen."

She didn't say anything, and I knew I had timed it right.

She was asleep.

CHAPTER FIFTEEN
Poppy

I WOKE UP alone, which wasn't at all surprising. But... the music was surprising. The tinny sound of a radio in the main room and the smell of coffee and food cooking were too. Sinead, I thought, sad that whatever time Ronan and I had was over.

But the dark outside the window was broken by the silvery light of a waning moon. It was still the middle of the night.

I stood and found the clothes we'd abandoned in front of the fire folded and stacked on the edge of the bed. The shirt he'd used to bind my wrists I tied it in a knot around my waist and went out into the main room.

Ronan was making food, something in a pot he was stirring, and humming along to music being played on the radio. Old Irish songs like in movies.

"Hi," I said.

"Sorry, did I wake you?"

"No." I smiled. "Not at all. Did you sleep?"

"No."

I stepped from the cold wood floor to the rug, rubbing the bottom of one foot on the top, wishing I had put on socks. "What time do we have to leave?"

"In about four hours. You should go back to bed."

"I'm not tired."

"You hungry?"

"Starving," I said. He smiled at my fierceness and pointed at a seat at the table. The coffee pot was on the table and I poured myself a cup.

"What are you listening to?"

"Sinead's radio gets one station. The oldies out of Derry. It's nothing but folk songs."

"It's nice."

"Nice is a stretch."

He laughed. It took me a second to reconcile all of this. This whole scene of him: shirtless in a pair of blank sweatpants hanging low on his hips, stirring a pot on the old stove. I realized what the sharp blade of him, which I had been sure made him cold all the way through, actually was. Protection. Fierce protection. For the people he decided to protect.

And himself.

With him around, no one would get close to me. But I would never get close to him.

He fussed around a little bit with the plate and what was coming out of the pot and a jar of red jam by the cutting board. "It's Sinead's specialty. It's not fancy but it will fill you up, like."

"Yeah?"

"Potato bread farl," he said. "One with beans. One with jam." He handed me the plate and then went back to get his own. Then he sat down next to me at the table. A knife and fork were in front of me, and I used them to scoop up some of the beans. Then had a bite of the bread.

"Did she make this for you a lot?" I asked, stepping carefully into unknown waters, expecting at any second for him to snap my hand off for trying. He'd destroyed me last night. Laid waste to the person I was. The conceptions I had about myself. I'd like to think I took a couple of chunks off him too. But I could never tell. Not with him.

"Once," he said. "One time. But she told me then that it was her specialty. Though, I figure she might have been lying."

The food was salty and rich and we both ate like it was the only thing that mattered.

"What was the one time?" I asked, and he shook his head without looking at me. Like he wasn't going to tell me that story. I pulled the bread, which was sort of flat and stretchy but tasted like butter and salt. I ate the edges around the jam.

"What are you doing?" he asked.

"Saving the best part for last. You don't do that?"

"God no." He laughed. Again. It was almost like I was dreaming. "Gives the assholes a chance to knick it. You've got to have the best part first or you'll never get it."

"Did you learn that at the school up there?"

"You're really fishing, aren't you?"

"If, in a few hours, we're never going to see each other again, what's the harm in telling me?"

"If, in a few hours, we're never going to see each other again, what's the point?" he fired back, his blue eyes shuttered.

I shrugged and set down the food. I wasn't hungry anymore and wasn't tired either. He ate quickly, the plate pulled close like at any moment it might get taken away. I remembered the way he'd eaten when we'd sat in that bullshit office Caroline had given me. He'd eaten like we were in a fine-dining restaurant. All manners and grace.

"I'm never going to understand you, much less know you, am I?"

He laughed once more over his food and then sat back with his cup of coffee. "Princess," he said. "I sincerely hope not."

"Has anyone?"

"Caroline," he said, surprising me. "She . . . knew me. Or a part of me, anyway. Or maybe she just made me feel like she knew me. Like the worst parts of me and . . . she thought they were admirable. Useful."

I think you're admirable, I almost said, but kept the words behind my teeth.

"But she just wanted . . . what did that Morelli call me? A junkyard dog?"

"She could have found one of those anywhere," I said. "I think she must have seen something special in you."

"That's because you still think something about Caroline is pure."

"Why else would she—?"

"I don't know," he said with a shrug, like it didn't matter, but I could tell it did. It had to.

"Why did we come here?" I asked, leaning back, my stomach full. Bold because I was running out of time to know him. And I wanted so badly to know him.

He stood, picking up his plate and taking mine back to the sink.

"Because no one would ever think to look here," he said. "Because it's the edge of the fucking world." The dishes clattered in the sink and he turned on the water. Abruptly, he turned it back off. "She was the only one who ever helped," he said. "That's why we're back here. Because Sinead, at huge cost to herself, when she found out what was going on up at the church, she raised bloody hell." He turned to face me, braced against the counter and the night sky outside the window. One lonely light on in the vestry window.

"Father McConal was running out of ways to punish Tommy. Nothing worked. He'd beat him and starve him. Wouldn't let him sleep. But then he'd found out that Tommy was feeding those fucking cats. Tommy loved those cats, Poppy. He'd named 'em. Fretted over 'em. Found any reason to help Father Patrick with the garden. But McConal found out and he had them all killed. Twenty cats. Can you believe it? Tommy went absolutely mad. Screaming and crying and promising to do anything. Total surrender, the one thing he'd promised he'd never do. But Father McConal didn't give a shit at that point.

He didn't care about Tommy's soul. He only wanted to hurt him. So, the cats were killed and two nights later, Tommy hung himself with a sheet in the bathrooms.

"Sinead had just moved into the cottage and she worked for the school, running kids back and forth to the village for appointments. She bought groceries and the like. And she was young and a single mom, and the priests had thought she needed the job and the home and the security enough that she wouldn't betray them. The night Tom died, I ran away down to Sinead's, planning to steal her car and get the fuck out of town. But she was standing on the path, staring up at the church. And she wasn't even surprised to see me, like. She looked at me and said, 'There's something bad happening at that church, isn't there?' And she brought me into her house and she fed me that farl with jam, and I told her what had happened to Tom. And she got her twelve year old daughter out of bed and we went into town. She went to the constable station and when they told her to fuck off, she went to the newspaper. I swear to God that night we drove around lighting up every journalist and chief constable she could get her hands on until someone believed her. Until someone promised to get things done."

"She got the school shut down?"

"She did. The journalists made such a fuss, the church had to do something. Father Patrick helped."

"Father Patrick, the man up there?" I asked.

He held out his hands, telling me to calm down. "Yeah, but he'd been at the school long enough. I doubt he would have done it if Sinead hadn't already risked everything."

"He asked you to forgive him."

He shrugged. "Some things don't get forgiven."

I stood and he braced himself like he knew I was going to approach him, but all I did was finish cleaning up the table. Clearing our coffee cups. Trying not to spook him. "You risked everything too. Telling Sinead."

"No. When we got to Derry, I took off, like. Found some old friends and started doing all the same shit that got me in trouble in the first place. I heard the school got shut down and Sinead got to keep the cottage. I didn't run away that night planning to do anything but save my own skin. And that's all I did for the next twelve years, whatever needed doing so I could survive."

"Until me."

He laughed. "Until you. And trust me, I've

learned my lesson. It won't happen again."

He turned back to the sink of dirty dishes. It was like seeing a wolf doing the washing up with its sharp claws.

"What's going to happen tomorrow?" I asked after a long moment.

"We'll get on a train to London."

"How are you affording all this? Jets, apartments, train tickets, new identities?" I sat back in the chair. "Are you rich?"

"Does it matter?'

In so many ways, it mattered a lot. But Ronan wouldn't be any less Ronan if he were rich or poor. He was impervious to such things. "I guess not. So, we get my sister in London, and then what?"

"You two lay low until it's safe for you to come back."

"If you go back, Caroline's not going to trust you."

"I should hope not."

"And the Morellis—"

"Need to answer for Theo Rivers. And I plan on finding out why anyone wants you dead."

"Or alive," I said, feeling like someone needed to keep saying that part out loud.

"Well, that part I get. You're not so bad

alive." As far as compliments went, it was pretty weak, but it's not like he'd said a lot of nice things to me over our brief relationship.

"You need to work on your flattery." I wished I could just reach out to touch him. The muscles in his back. The scar there along his jaw. How exciting it would be to have the right to touch him. How exciting it would be for him to be mine.

"You're doing all of that to make it safe for me?"

"Yeah."

"But that can't be safe for you."

"Not much is, Poppy."

So, he was going to go back to make things safe for me and I was going to sit in a house in England that he paid for while waiting for him to come out. It hardly seemed fair. Or right.

"How do I repay you?" I asked. "I mean . . . Ronan? How do I possibly repay you for any of this?"

He turned so fast, I blinked. Stepped back. He crowded me against the counter, his hands braced on either side, dripping water onto the floor. His eyes walked all over my face, like he was soaking me in. Memorizing me. "You never should have been in this life, Poppy. You want to repay me? Live the life you were supposed to have. Just be happy, Poppy."

I couldn't stand him so close, yet even a breath away, he was too far away. I leaned forward, kissing him. With all the sweetness I had in me. All the sweetness I felt for him. The sweetness I wished for him.

I knew he would only allow that for so long before changing the kiss. Taking all its brightness and making it dark. Making it his. He put his arms around my waist and lifted me off my feet, carrying me into the bedroom where he wouldn't have sex with me. Where he wouldn't love me.

And I had never felt so loved.

CHAPTER SIXTEEN

Ronan

This was the last time, and the nature of last times meant they seemed more important. Gilded, maybe. Special. When they weren't. I'd had a lifetime of last times, and I knew the last time I'd seen my da alive wasn't any more special than any other time I'd watched him, shoulders hunched against the cold drizzle on his way to the pub to drink away all the things he needed to drink away.

So this, I had to remind myself as I kissed Poppy—her body so soft and giving under mine—only seemed special because my brain was playing a trick on me.

Last times, first times—it was all context.

I swept her hair back with my hands and felt the damp from the corners of her eyes to her hairline. I pressed my lips there and she tried to pull away, but I tasted the salt of her tears.

"Poppy," I breathed, shifting away from her,

but she held on, pulling me back.

"Don't," she said, shaking her head even as more tears fell. "Don't stop."

"I don't mess around with crying women, Poppy."

"I'm not crying."

"Poppy."

She attached herself to my body like a monkey, arms and legs wrapping around me. God, she was small against me.

"Please," she whispered against my ear, sucking the lobe into her mouth and then biting with the force she somehow instinctively knew was the perfect amount. I swallowed my gasp and pleasure rippled through my body.

"Please. I want you inside me. I need you inside me, Ronan."

"No, Poppy."

She reached between us, her hand curling around my cock. This was the fucking problem with last times. They were loaded propositions. The pull of useless emotion was impossible to resist. Even I felt it and I was hardened against such things. But her hand on my cock was delicious. The feel of her against my body was undeniable, and even I understood I would be thinking about this moment for a long time.

Missing her when I shouldn't.

"Does it bother you?" she asked, stroking me. Squeezing the tip, rubbing the head with her thumb. "That I'm going to be asking a man to fuck me and he'll do it? He'll do it and it won't be you?"

Fuck. This fucking girl. Always wanting more. Always wanting what she shouldn't have. I would think, having lived through the pain she'd lived through, the lessons would be learned. But here she was: a woman bartered away and raped by her husband, manipulated by me, and wanted dead or alive by people who could make the worst happen.

How did she still manage to want more? To have hope?

"Please, Ronan. We would feel so good—"

I knocked away her hand and rolled on top of her, spreading her legs out wide. So wide it had to hurt. But I pressed the hard length of my cock against her clit and rocked against her. In the burst of pleasure between us, I could see what she wanted. How she was hoping tomorrow wouldn't come.

"Open your eyes, Poppy."

She did as I asked because she would do anything I asked. I stared down at her with the icy cold distance I surrounded myself with. Even now. Pressed up hard against her, her body's welcome slick against my cock. Even here I could bring it up because I had to. Because this was survival.

"This game you're playing—"

"It's not a game."

"Well, it's not real. There's no world where we are an us."

Silent, she looked up at me, and I could see her biting her tongue. "You're making everything harder," I said. "For yourself. Tomorrow, you'll regret this because everything goes back the way it was."

"Where you pretend you don't care and—"

"I don't fucking care." I said it right to her face.

"I don't believe you," she said, fierce through her tears. She curled her leg around me and used her weight to roll us over. "You know what I'm going to do?"

"Leave me and never look back?"

"No."

It's not like I couldn't push her off me. End this in some blunt manner. Leaving would be smart because the lesson she needed to learn was a cold one. But this was the fucking last time, and I couldn't not feel it. Couldn't not feel *her*.

"I'm going to ruin you, Ronan," she said, spreading her thighs over my hips. Slipping me, just a little, inside of her body. My hands caught her waist, holding her still. One inch of my cock dipped in lava. I wasn't fucking her; I wasn't *not* fucking her.

"Oh my God," she gasped as the head of my cock stretched her wide. She'd had my fingers and been tight around them.

My brain was short-circuiting, and my body wanted so much more, but I held her there. Every muscle shaking. The tip of my cock bathed in fire.

"Oh my God. It's good like I thought. Just like I thought." Her eyes pinned me to the bed. "I'll leave tomorrow and maybe I'll never see you again. But you're going to go back to your cold life and every woman you meet, every woman you touch—you're going to wish they were me."

She said it like that hadn't been true since she'd stepped out into the side yard at the party. Since the moment I'd met her.

She rocked back and forth, and my hold on her weakened. She took another inch of me. She was slick and ready but still small, and my cock was far bigger than my fingers. She winced as she stretched, and that wince was like a cold shower.

I am only an instrument of pain, and my only job was to protect her.

This wasn't protecting her.

My hands on her waist lifted her. My cock slipped free. She arched, trying to get it back.

Her eyes met mine. She knew what I was doing, and she'd begged before without swaying me. She'd taken two inches of me inside her body, claimed it for herself. But I could give her no more. Not without hurting her.

I repositioned her over my body so my hard cock pressed against her clit. She twitched and arched, fucking herself against me.

Poppy closed her eyes as if the sight of me was too much, and I watched her every move. Her every facial expression. I drank down her cries and her sobs. Her sighs and her screams.

While she burned me to the ground. I filled myself up with her.

We held each other, kissed each other—too hard. We made it hurt all the way up until the second it was pleasure.

I pushed her and pushed her until she begged to come, and then shaking and sobbing, she begged me to stop.

The ruin happened to both of us.

I had hard callouses on my hands. A thousand

scars. My thumbnail was all fucked up from getting stepped on by some bloke in a fight. I had no nerve endings in two fingers on my right hand from grabbing the business end of a knife. Callouses were good. Solid reminders of who I was. Of the kind of man I was.

A hard man. A killer. The kind of man who did the work that needed doing. I hadn't second-guessed it or thought about it in years. I'd known in my father's house exactly who I was. And everything after that just built up the callouses.

Poppy had no callouses. She was nothing but soft skin looking to get hurt. And this next part—it was going to hurt her.

A lot.

Because at the end of this, she needed to not look back at me. She needed to run from me like I was the threat. Because I was. All this shit for the last few days didn't change that I was the worst thing for her. That I was the part of her life most likely to get her hurt.

Or killed.

And to prevent that—well, it was time to build some callouses.

I pulled myself out of the bed and into another shower. I dressed in my own clothes that Sinead had laundered, made a fresh pot of coffee, stared out the windows, and made more plans.

Plans four levels deep. Contingencies and emergencies.

- If Zilla wasn't in the house in London.
- If Zilla was, but she'd been found by the Morellis or, perhaps worse, the Constantines.
- If I'd blown the window and someone from either of those families had figured out where we were and heading into the village in an hour was the equivalent of walking into an ambush.
- If Poppy refused to be left at the safe house.

This was how I used to operate until Poppy came in and distracted me. It was how a man stayed alive in my line of work. And with every plan, every step I made in my head away from her, I found myself settling back into the man I'd been. The cold dark in the back of my brain took over and I let it be the only thing that mattered.

I had one job: Poppy's survival. And I was the greatest risk to her.

She had to break—her heart had to break—so she could be stronger. And if I had to do it, then I would.

When the edge of the eastern sky turned pink, I stood in the doorway to the bedroom with a focused mind and scar-tissue heart.

CHAPTER SEVENTEEN

POPPY

I DREAMED ABOUT my sister. We were at the top of the sledding hill in Bishop's Landing. Snow had gotten in between her boot and the bare skin of her leg and she was crying that it hurt. I was trying to scoop it out with my mittened hands, aware her reaction to this snow was . . . a lot. Too much, maybe.

"Calm down," I said. "I'll get it, but you need to be still."

"It feels like fire!" she kept yelling, tears pouring down her pink cheeks. Mom had a headache and sent us out the door, telling us not to come back until it started to get dark. Which was hours away. Zilla had been like this all day, overreacting and wild. It was a little scary. This was happening more and more; her reactions to things, always big, were now unpredictable. I didn't ever seem to say the right thing to calm her down. Mom sent us out because Zilla exhausted her, and I hated to admit it, but Zilla scared me.

The snow was melting against the heat of her leg and my fingers, and the cold water was dripping further down her sock. She moaned and made a big deal out of it.

"Zilla! You're overreacting."

"No, I'm not. You just don't know how it feels. You've never been hurt like this."

"*Poppy.*"

"I'm trying, Zilla."

"*Poppy! Wake up!*"

I shot up in bed, the sheets falling to my waist, the cold air a full body slap.

Ronan stood in the doorway, dressed in his long jacket and the dark jeans he'd worn the night I'd gotten shot. His face was hard. Cruel. He looked so much like the man from Bishop's Landing. The man who felt nothing but pity and disdain for me.

"Ronan," I said, refusing to lift the sheets. Refusing to cower in front of his suddenly cold gaze.

"Get up. We need to get moving."

The sky was just turning pink and gray, and the sound outside the cottage was nothing but crashing waves, like the weather was coming in. A storm.

I splashed water on my face and my body and then dressed in the fresh leggings and long, soft, flannel shirt that had been left for me. Still no underwear. Really made a girl on the run feel extra naked.

In the main room, he stood with a cup of coffee and turned when I walked out. He looked at me slowly, taking in my hair and clothes.

"You really look different," he said.

"I thought that was the point."

He sucked in a deep breath as if something he hadn't thought of just occurred to him.

"What?"

"We need to get going. Put on your boots."

"You're not even going to talk to me?" I asked as he walked past me to the door. "Shouldn't I know the plan?"

"I just changed it. I'll fill you in on the drive." Then he was gone.

Well, fuck that guy, I thought, without a lot of heat. I'd known, of course, that he was going to do this. Retreat or whatever. That took some of the edge off his words, but not all of it.

I took my time saying goodbye to Rascal, who purred while I stroked her ears and then, true to form, attacked me.

"Ouch, okay. You damn cat," I muttered,

shaking the cat off my hand until she let go and then immediately climbed onto the highest part of the chair. She settled herself in with a good purr. "You," I told the animal. "Are a lot like him."

It was a tiny rebellion, and perhaps a stupid one considering the stakes of the day, but I took the time to find a mug in the way back of the cupboard and poured myself a cup of coffee. I then found a piece of paper and a pen and wrote Sinead a quick note.

Thank you. I took a mug; I'll try and get it back to you. And the clothes. Thank you.

What a completely inadequate thank you card, but what was the etiquette for a woman who gave up her cottage so you could hide from the two families who wanted to kill you? Maybe I'd send some flowers when I got settled.

I took one last look around, grateful to this tiny place for its warmth. I'd rattled around giant homes for most of my life and never once felt at home in them. My future home would be something more like this. Small and safe and comfortable. Just for me and my sister and no one else.

Though, initially, that place would be Ronan's, so what the hell did I know?

I went out to the car, shutting the cottage's

door behind me. The wind caught my hair and pushed me sideways until I leaned into it and opened the car's passenger side door and climbed in.

"I took a mug," I said. "I hate taking her mug, but I took the one with a chip in it, so I hope it's not special."

Silent, he started the car.

"We're just leaving? We're not going to say goodbye to Sinead or Father—?"

"You need to understand it's best for everyone if they don't know when you left or where you're going."

"Why?"

"So if someone comes looking for information, it can't be beaten out of them."

"Oh," I said stupidly.

Did someone ever get used to being a threat to the people in their lives? I could maybe ask Ronan, but he didn't seem very chatty this morning. I settled into the seat and directed the vents away from me. "So, what's this new plan?"

He took the left turn fast and I had to brace myself against the door so I didn't slosh coffee all over myself. "Jesus, Ronan."

"I'm going to put you on the bus in the village. The bus will take you to Carrickfergus and from there, you'll get the train down to London."

"By myself?"

"By yourself?"

I wished that didn't make me scared. I really wished I were tougher than that, but it would be a lie. This new plan was terrifying. "Why are we doing this? Is it because of last night?" Was he punishing me for trying to fuck him the way I had? Truthfully, I felt bad about it. Like I'd taken something from he didn't want to give, even though he didn't really fuck me. He'd been inside of me just a little and not for long. Between my legs, I was tender and sore and all I wanted was more. "I'm sorry that I forced the—"

"No."

I waited for something more from him. Some sign of the man who'd made me farl with jam and beans. But he wasn't in the car with us today.

"But . . . what about you? We were going to go together. The two of us."

"You don't look like the person they're looking for."

"That's good right?"

"But I do."

I pursed my lips at him. "We should have dyed your hair. Put you in some flannel."

He was silent.

"So . . . that's it? Really?"

"I'll give you the address in London. You've got to memorize it, like, and we'll buy you a burner phone in the village. You'll be with your sister by sunset."

That sounded good. But not good enough to change my heartache over this goodbye. I sipped my coffee, and he drove too fast, and knowing something was coming and wanting it to come had never been such two separate things before. It was harder than I thought to hold them both in my hands.

The village was dark; rows and rows of small and connected houses lined cobblestone roads. Dogs at the ends of chains barked as we went by. There was a castle in the distance, lit up and a little menacing. I wanted to ask Ronan about it, but the man driving the car was a little menacing too. So, I concentrated on not spilling my coffee and seeing my sister.

Ronan turned onto a downhill road that led to the harbor with boats bobbing in a marina. There were small stretches of businesses on either side of the road. Bakeries and coffee shops and chippys and clothing stores. Ronan pulled into a grocery parking lot.

"Sit tight," he said and left.

I sat in the quiet car watching a few early shoppers stroll past, in and out of the brightly lit doors of the grocery. One of the people, a man, stopped by the car and knocked on the passenger side window.

I jumped and screamed in my throat.

"Open the window," he said to me through the glass. He wore a cap pulled down low so I couldn't see his face and his hands were in the pockets of his thick coat.

Morellis, I thought. *Dead or alive.*

I threw my leg over the gear shift, climbing from the passenger seat to the driver's seat.

He leaned down, glaring at me through the window. "I have paperwork. For Ronan?" The words didn't register. I had my hand on the door handle, thinking I could run.

"Jaysus," the guy said and then opened the passenger side door, tossing a big envelope from under his jacket onto the seat. It all happened so fast I didn't even have time to begin this scream.

He gave me a rude gesture through the windshield and walked on like nothing had happened, and I laughed so I wouldn't cry out of fear.

I picked up the envelope and tipped it over into the seat. A deep red passport slipped out, as well as a driver's license and a bank card. All with the picture Ronan had taken of me in the cottage bedroom.

My hair looked like a five year old had cut it and without makeup on, my face was almost completely washed out. I didn't even have eyebrows. But perhaps the strangest difference was the set of my jaw and the look in my eyes.

Yeah. The woman staring back at me—Beth Soeterick of Brussels—was a stranger. Even to me.

Ronan opened the door and found me sitting in his seat. I scrambled back over to the passenger side.

"Glenn came?" he asked looking at the passport in my hand.

"Yeah. Scared me."

"I should have warned you, but I thought he'd come find me in the store. He must have recognized you from the picture."

"The picture doesn't look like me at all." I showed him the driver's license. He glanced at the confident stranger and back up at me.

"Yeah, it does."

"I mean, the hair and whatever, but she looks—"

His eyes met mine. "Exactly like you." He handed me a phone. "Here you go. New sim card. New number. It will work in London; but if you go in the EU, you'll need something new."

"Can I call my sister?"

"You can try the house," he said, and I punched in the number as he gave it to me. I pressed the phone to my ear and my fingers to my lips and prayed. *Please, please let my sister—*

"Hello?"

I closed my eyes with a sob. "Zilla?"

"Holy shit, Pops. I mean—holy shit. Where the fuck are you?"

Ronan touched my arm and shook his head.

"I . . . I can't tell you. But I'll be there tonight."

"Here? At this fucking house?"

"Yes."

"Oh, thank God! Oh, thank fucking God! Do you know what's going on? Like . . . at all?"

"No. I mean, a little. I'll explain what I can when I get there."

"Has she seen anyone around?" Ronan asked. "Anything strange."

"Ronan wants to know if there's been anything strange there?"

"Other than everything? It's like I'm living in a very swanky, very posh jail. With gourmet food and a steam shower."

"That doesn't sound too bad." So much for

my bad apartment in a sky rise vision.

"It's weird, Poppy."

"Everything is weird right now. But I'll see you in a few hours."

Ronan gestured that it was time to cut the call short and I said my goodbyes and hung up, pressing the hard plastic to my lips.

I felt him looking at me. Maybe he wanted to say something. Comfort me. The guy from the last few days at the cottage would have done that. Would have tried, anyway. But that guy was gone.

"Get me on the damn bus," I said, turning away to wipe my eyes.

Saying nothing, he started the car and we drove away from the grocery store. "Are you hungry?" he asked. "The train's an hour ride—"

"I'm fine."

More silence.

"You have money in the bank account." He reached into his pocket and pulled out a thick stack of cash. The kind you only ever saw in movies. "Here's another five grand."

"Five grand?" I cried. "Where do I put all of this? I don't have a purse."

"We'll get you something near the bus. Put it all in the envelope for now."

Five grand and a bunch of fake IDs. I'd never

been so criminal in my life. "When are you going back to the States?"

"I have a flight tonight."

"Isn't that dangerous? Booking a flight—"

"I'm flying in a private jet. No one knows I'm coming."

"Private jets, secret houses, money like this? You are rich, aren't you?"

"Being a very bad monster pays very well, Poppy."

He smiled at me and it was like getting punched in the chest. "Will . . . will I ever see you again?"

He turned the wheel, pulling us alongside the curb. The bus depot was ahead.

"If we see each other again, Poppy, it's because something has gone wrong in my plan. So, I sincerely hope this is the last you see of me."

CHAPTER EIGHTEEN

Poppy

I COULDN'T SINCERELY hope that, but I nodded because there was nothing to say.

He reached forward, his fingers touching my cheek, and I flinched away. "Don't make it worse," I whispered.

He nodded as if he understood and then he got out of the car. It took me a second to put everything in my envelope and then I followed too. He stood ahead of me on the sidewalk, waiting for me. Beside him was a shop with backpacks on a rack outside the door. In the window were coats, another thing I needed. I wondered if I might find some underwear too.

"I'm going to stop in here," I said. "I'll be a few minutes."

"All right," he said and jerked his thumb back at the depot. "I'll get you a ticket."

He walked away and I sucked in a deep shuddery breath.

The future, Poppy, I reminded myself. *Think of the future. Zilla. School.*

I opened the door, and behind all the racks of coats and backpacks and purses, a woman said, "Be with you in a moment," in a singsong voice. I couldn't see her because the store was stuffed full. I had to push sideways between coats and sweaters. There was a whole section of kids' bathing suits and beach umbrellas and towels.

"Do you have any women's underwear?" I asked, stepping deeper into the store, nearly knocking over a display of sunglasses.

The woman didn't answer.

She must be in the store room or something, I thought, and pulled out a deep green sweatshirt with a hood and big pockets in the front. I also grabbed a black backpack and a smaller purse.

I crouched down and kind of duck walked between two stuffed coat racks. Lo and behold, there were some very sad packages of women's underwear. I grabbed a three pack of black bikinis and a sports bra that looked like it might fit.

"I found some!" I cried to the woman in the back in case she could hear me and then I dragged myself and my stuff through the tiny shop to the cash register that was in the back of the store.

The woman wasn't in the storeroom. She

stood stone still behind the register. Eyes closed with tears streaming down her face. A man beside her held a gun to her head.

I stumbled backward only to run into someone.

Ronan!

But it wasn't Ronan. It was a dark-haired man with olive skin and a nose that had been smashed more than once.

"You're not an easy woman to find, Poppy Maywell," he said with a thick New York accent.

"I'm B-Beth," I stammered. "Soeterick."

His smile was a mockery. "You're mine, is what you are. Let's go." He grabbed the elbow of my bad shoulder so hard I whimpered, and at the sound of my whimper, the girl behind the counter, hardly older than a teenager, started to cry in earnest.

"Please," she begged. "Please, just let me go. Don't—"

"Shut her the fuck up!" the man holding my elbow said to the man with the gun.

"Don't hurt her!" I cried. "Don't—!" A muffled gunshot pierced in the air around me, and the girl went ominously silent. I screamed in my throat even as the guy grabbed me around the head, his hand over my mouth.

"You, they want alive, but loose ends are nothing but trouble." He started to pull me through the back, around the counter, to a shadowy doorway that must lead to a back entrance. We had to walk past the body of the shop girl who lay in a heap, her pretty red hair covering her face.

I'm sorry, I thought. *I'm so sorry.*

I tripped on a step and the guy carrying me cursed. In my panic, I somehow realized if they planned on taking me alive, then I could fight. I had to fight.

I grabbed onto the doorway with both hands, my shoulder screaming in pain, stitches popping as I tried to pull myself free. I yanked him off balance, but all he did was wrench me backward off my feet.

I was a barrage of elbows and kicks. If he was going to take me, I wasn't going to make it easy.

We made it out into the back alley, bleak and gray where there was a dark van waiting for me. There was no way I was getting into that van. No way.

I bit him so hard I tasted blood.

"You fucking bitch!" he muttered and turned me by my shoulders, his hand off my mouth. I got just enough breath to scream "Ronan!" before he hauled off and punched me in the stomach so hard, I buckled forward, all the air knocked out of me. I couldn't breathe. I couldn't get my body to work. My vision went sparkly and black. I fell onto the slick stones of the alley.

"Dead or alive, bitch!" Smash Nose said to me. "That's the hit order, and you keep up with that shit, they can get you dead." He picked me up under my arms and I was sipping at air, my head swimming.

Distantly, there was a scuffle. Or perhaps it was just my feet dragging across the stones as he pulled me toward the van. The side door open.

"No," I wheezed, trying still to fight.

There was a pop and then a thud, and I collapsed back onto the ground.

"What?" Smash Nose said, turning toward the front of the van. Ronan stood there, like some angel of death. A spray of blood was across his face.

"Hey!" Smash Nose said. "We found her first. This is our bounty—"

Ronan lifted his gun and shot Smash Nose in the head. The hit man toppled backward and fell over my leg, cracking open what was left of his skull. I kicked him off me, crawling across the stones to get away from the growing pool of blood, and then Ronan was there, lifting me to my feet.

"Can you breathe?" he asked, holding my head, staring me right in the eyes. Shock and a cramped diaphragm made the answer a solid no. I shook my head.

"With me, Poppy." He took a deep breath and I gasped. "Breathe with me."

Another deep breath from him, his eyes on mine. His hands holding me. His chest as it rose touched mine, and I took a breath deeper than a gasp. Again, and then again.

Once I could properly breathe, he stepped away from me. "You all right? Your shoulder?"

There was blood trickling down my arm, but not much I could do about it.

"Fine," I said and without another word, he grabbed me by the hand, pulling me toward the end of the alley. "But I dropped the money. The ID."

He shook his head. "Doesn't matter now. They've found us."

We ran down the alley to the side street. He stopped, edging around the building, his gun at his side.

"They . . . were . . . with the Morellis," I told him.

"There was another guy at the bus station," Ronan said.

"What are we going to do?"

"Get in the car and drive."

"Ronan," I whispered. "They killed the girl in the shop. They shot her."

"I know."

"We have to do something—"

"We have to survive, Poppy. Let's go."

We ran down the sidewalk to our shitty little car. We both opened the door and threw ourselves into the front seats.

"Buckle up," Ronan said, turning on the car.

"Yes," purred a voice from the back seat. "We wouldn't want anyone to get hurt."

Ronan spun, gun in hand, but I felt the cold press of a gun barrel against the skin of my nape.

"Hello, Poppy."

Carefully, with my hands up, I turned. In the back seat of the car, in a fur coat and a fresh blowout, was Eden Morelli.

CHAPTER NINETEEN

Ronan

I HAD NO idea who the woman was in the back seat was, but Poppy clearly did.

I cocked my gun, and she shook her head at me. "If you shoot me, I'm afraid my man over there will be forced to shoot you. And this whole thing will get so messy."

She pointed out the front window, and a man in a dark coat and ball cap was leaning against the car in front of us, a Beretta M9 with a silencer in his hand held across his chest.

I didn't know his name, but I recognized him. Junkyard dog. Same as me.

Fuck. I'd pooched this but good. I'd gotten soft. Poppy had made me soft, and I'd walked right into a goddamned trap.

"Eden," Poppy gasped, "what are you doing?"

Ah, this was the mysterious Morelli who'd told Poppy all about me. I could kill her just for that.

"Well, believe it or not, I'm trying to save your life."

"Must be why you're holding a gun on her," I snarled.

Eden smiled at me, her eyes skating across my face to the gun I held on her. "This is the world we live in, Ronan Byrne. I'm just trying to get by."

I very nearly laughed.

"Here's what we're going to do," she said. "You are going to drive us back to whatever hidey-hole you've been playing house in and my associate—" Again she pointed at the man in front of us. "Is going to clean up this mess and take care of any other people in town who are looking to cash in on the money my family has put on this girl's head."

"How much money?" Poppy asked.

"Enough that the Dubrassi Brothers are interested."

I swore under my breath and Poppy next to me went on high alert. "What does that mean? Is that bad? That sounds bad."

It was a "we needed more guns" kind of bad.

In the back seat, Eden turned to look at Poppy, specifically at her hair, and she could not contain her horror. "What happened to you?"

Self-consciously, Poppy touched her hair. "It's not that bad."

"No," Eden said. "It's worse, honey. It's so much worse."

"I'm not taking you anywhere," I said. "Fuck you and your goon."

Eden winced. "Goon? That's not very nice. But let me be clear—I have the solution for your Morelli problem."

"You do?" Poppy asked, sounding foolishly hopeful.

"Don't," I snapped.

"Don't what?" Poppy asked.

"He doesn't want you to hope," Eden said. "He thinks I'm lying. And fair enough. But the Morelli family has your sister's phone. She'd dumped it, but not very well. And that Good Samaritan Father Patrick inadvertently put a target on this area, so there are at least four teams of cold-blooded mercenaries who are coming to get Poppy. Dead or alive. Including, I repeat, the fucking Dubrassi Brothers. So, how about we go someplace quiet, and I'll tell you what I know?"

She didn't even finish her little speech before I gunned the engine and peeled away from the curb.

"You have a solution?" I asked her in the

rearview mirror.

"Fixing problems is kind of my thing."

Funny, I thought. *It used to be mine.*

"And your guy is going to clean up?" I asked.

"It's what he does."

She sat back and lowered her sunglasses down over her eyes, sitting there like a minor celebrity with a hangover.

"This car is a piece of shit," she said.

Poppy turned in her seat and looked back at Eden. "Why are you doing this? Why are you helping me?"

"Well, let's just say I have my own problem and I think we can help each other."

Loaded silence filled the car, the heavy kind, all of us thinking our own doomsday thoughts. The Dubrassi Brothers were a concern. This wild card in the back seat was a concern.

"Is my sister safe?" Poppy asked.

Zilla was a concern. So many goddamned concerns.

"No one knows where she is."

My London safe house was still secure, at least.

Poppy heaved a sigh of relief. "Thank God."

"For the moment," Eden added. "The longer you're missing, the more desperate people will get.

Holding her hostage to force you out of hiding is, I'm sure, going to be discussed."

I wanted to tell Eden to shut the fuck up, to stop scaring Poppy. But all of this was true and the disservice I'd done by not thinking about the worst-case scenario, not telling Poppy about the worst-case scenario, was painfully clear.

We'd been living in make-believe in that cottage.

"So," Eden said. "This is Ireland. It's a little bleak, isn't it?"

Make-believe was over.

CHAPTER TWENTY
Poppy

IT WAS HARD to keep up. Every time I closed my eyes, trying to keep the people straight in my head, I saw that poor shop girl on the floor. Her pretty hair over her face.

I would figure out who her family was and I'd tell them what happened. I'd give them money. Which was probably insulting. It *was* insulting. What was I going to do? How in the world could I fix this?

Without warning, I wished for my old life. The bird-in-a-cage one. At least the only person who'd gotten hurt in that life was me. I could handle that. Out here in this new world, I kept hurting people.

"Hey," Ronan said as we pulled up in front of the cottage. We'd gone the long way, Ronan checking over his shoulder all the time to see if we were being followed. "Stay here."

I nodded and watched him go into the cottage, gun in hand, on hyperalert.

"Jesus, he's even hotter than I'd heard," Eden said, sticking her head up between the seats. "It's the accent, right? That's a man. Have you fucked him? Because I would like to see that."

When I looked at her, mouth agape, she winked.

"You're taking all this life-or-death danger pretty well," I said, my voice cracking.

"It's kind of my natural habitat. I'm not sure what would happen to me if the heat were off."

Ronan came back out and opened my car door, still looking around. Still so vigilant. The guy he'd been the last twenty-four hours, listening to oldies and petting cats—he was truly so gone, it was like I'd made him up.

"Come on," he said, standing at the door. "The two of you."

Sore, I climbed out of the car and stood there, the steel and glass of the car door between us.

"You should get in the car and drive," I said to him. He looked at me, startled, before looking back at the horizon, scanning for threats. "This is my problem. Not yours. You should go now before it's too late."

"Oh, it's already too late," Eden said, walking into the cottage.

"She's right," Ronan said. "Let's go."

Inside, the cat was standing on the back of the chair snarling at Eden. Who was pointing her gun at it.

"Someone do something with this cat before I shoot it."

"Shhh," I said and grabbed Rascal who scratched and twisted in my arms until I dropped her. She ran into the bedroom, slinking under the bed.

"Tell me there's a proper drink here." Eden looked around, her fur coat behind her like the train on a monarch's cape.

I'd just left this place, but it seemed foreign. Maybe it was shock.

Or maybe it was just Eden Morelli.

"How about you tell us what you know," Ronan said. Both still had their guns in their hands, and I wondered if they were for each other or for the threat that was coming for us.

"Was it stupid coming back here?" I asked. "Aren't we just sitting ducks? We should have kept running."

"If you run now," Eden said. "You'll always be running—ah!" she cried, having found the bottle of Jameson on the counter. "There she is." She cracked the top and pulled three teacups out of the cupboard.

Two of the teacups got a reasonable amount of whiskey and the third got quite a bit more. She handed Ronan and me the smaller doses. Ronan ignored the cup, staring at Eden until she set the cup down on the table. I guzzled mine down.

"'Atta girl," Eden said with a wink and then tossed hers back too. She poured us each another.

"Jesus Christ," Ronan muttered. "Can we get on with things?"

"Of course." She lifted her teacup and drank her second shot. I left mine on the table. "Now. You might want to sit down for this."

With weak knees, I sat. Ronan, of course, did not, so Eden sat in the chair across from me. Ronan stood with his back to the fireplace so he could look out the front and back windows.

"Why do they want me dead or alive?" I asked.

Eden sat back, her legs crossed. She pulled the fur around her like a blanket. "Well, it's partly because of Caroline. Her pet and her monster out in the world together? That's too tempting for the Morellis to resist."

"Then why don't they want me dead or alive?" Ronan asked.

"Because they think she knows something."

"Me?"

"Yes. You."

"What do they think I know? Because I don't know anything. I swear to God—"

"Look, honey, I believe you. But you were married to the senator and the senator worked for the Morellis."

"No," I said, "he worked for Caroline."

"He worked for both of them?" Ronan asked and Eden put her finger on her nose.

"Ding-ding, give that boy a prize."

"That explains the alive part but not the dead part," Ronan said, and I was really getting tired of being talked about this way.

Eden shrugged. "What they think she knows, they don't want anyone else knowing."

"I swear," I said. "I don't know anything."

"Well, lucky for you, I know how to get you out of this little jam you're in."

"Little jam." That was one way of putting it.

"Okay. How—how do I get out?"

"You need to come back," she said.

"To New York?"

"Nope." Ronan shook his head. "No way—"

"Yep. To New York. With him." Eden said, pointing at Ronan.

We all blinked at each other.

"Why me?" he asked. "I'm no one."

"Yeah." Eden pursed her very full lips. "Actually. You are someone. You're kind of a big-deal someone. And I think for the rest of this conversation, I'd feel a whole lot better if you weren't holding that gun."

"Too bad," he said, staring her down.

She reached over, grabbed his teacup of whiskey, and drank it down. "Your mother died just after giving birth to you—"

"What the fuck?" he snapped. "How do you know that?"

"Please, just . . . listen." Eden actually looked nervous, which made me nervous. "Your parents never married. They, from what I understand, barely knew each other. Do you know where they met?"

"Da never talked about her."

"Your mother worked at a pub in East London, near where your father worked as a food packer. Your mom had just gotten to London and got the job through a friend of hers. A girl she'd gone to boarding school with in the States."

"Boarding school?" Ronan asked, like he didn't understand the words. But I knew that what he was really struggling with was that boarding school meant money. And he grew up poor.

"Knowing things is how I've managed to survive the Morelli family, though that's currently being tested. But it's also not the point. Yet. I think there's a good chance your father might not have known any of this either."

"And that's why he didn't talk about her?" Ronan asked.

"She was in London for six months and then ended up pregnant. Your father attempted to do the right thing, but she wouldn't marry him. Apparently, she thought she'd go back to the States at some point, and a baby was okay, but she didn't want to encumber herself with a cranky Irishman with a drinking problem."

Ronan leveled the gun at Eden's face. "I'm going to ask you one more time; how do you know all of this?"

"I wasn't born a Morelli. I married Maxim, Bryant's oldest brother. He was three times my age and richer than God with one foot in the grave when I met him—my kind of dreamboat. He kept himself out of the Constantine–Morelli drama that his brother was knee-deep in. He thought it was all a little pedestrian."

"Sounds like a real gem. What the fuck does that have to do with me?"

"I'm getting there," she said with her hands up. Ronan had advanced across the room. He looked like a killer, and Eden, for the first time, had the good sense to be scared. "His youngest sister was the white sheep in a black sheep family, you know? She was above the money and not interested in the crime. She wanted to travel and see the world and find her own way. She was told if she left, she'd be disowned, and being disowned is a thing the Morelli family does not play around with. When you're out, you're dead to them. But the second she could, she left anyway. First stop: London."

For an instant, it was like my entire body was tied to Ronan's. Like when we were in bed together. I knew how he felt, what he was thinking, because I was feeling and thinking the same things. The sudden blast of shock made my entire body numb.

"What are you saying?" Ronan asked.

"Her name was Gwen. Gwen Morelli."

"You're fucking lying!" Ronan yelled and I stood, finding a place between Ronan and Eden.

"Ronan," I whispered, my eye on that gun. I was only a little convinced he would not shoot me. "Please—"

"My mother was not a Morelli," he said. "I'm

not a fucking Morelli."

From the pocket of her fur coat, Eden pulled out a piece of paper that had been folded into a small square. She unfolded it and spread it flat. Ronan reached forward and grabbed it. "What the fuck is this?"

"Look," Eden said as calmly as she could. "It's all right there."

I could see it over his shoulder. It was his birth certificate. Father: Sean Byrne. Mother: Gwen Morelli.

"Oh my god," I whispered.

"This is fake," Ronan said, rejecting it.

"Why would I fake it?" Eden asked.

"I don't know why you're doing any of this."

"Your file," I whispered and pointed at the blue folder on the mantel. "You said it had your birth certificate in it."

He dropped the paper Eden had given him and grabbed the folder. Eden stood, gathered the teacups, and went to refill them as if she were just hosting a little party. But it also indicated how confident she was that she was right.

"Holy . . ." Ronan finally turned to look at me, his eyes wide and full of so much pain. "It's true. I'm a Morelli."

CHAPTER TWENTY-ONE
Ronan

ODDLY, IT ANSWERED a question that had been bothering me for years. Why me? Why did Caroline Constantine pick me up out of the gutters when they were so full of boys exactly like me? Why did she install me at her side? What was special about me?

I had thought, perhaps, it was my blind loyalty. My willingness to do whatever she wanted. Needed. Those things had value.

But this was the answer.

Because I was the child of her enemy. She'd groomed me. Trained me. Used me against her enemy. My family.

It was so diabolical. It was genius. The laughter that poured out of me—like water from a broken kettle—was tinged with madness.

The breath in and out of my body crackled and burned. Eden handed me a teacup full of whiskey and I drank it this time. Poppy tried to touch my arm and I shrugged it off.

"How long has the Morelli family known about this?" I asked.

"Not long," Eden said and then adjusted her coat around her body. "I . . . ah . . . I just told them."

"Why?" I asked.

"How do you know?" Poppy asked at the same time, but that was hardly relevant anymore. We were past that. But Poppy didn't fully realize what was happening. She had a few more seconds of innocence.

"Well, Bryant was getting a little tired of my . . . sharing of Morelli secrets and was threatening to disown me."

"You're dragging me into this because you don't want to lose your furs?" I asked.

"Well, it gets a little uglier than that. Morellis don't kill Morellis. And if I were no longer a Morelli . . ." She shrugged, the fur slipping off her shoulder.

"He would kill you?" Poppy asked, shocked.

"She really is an innocent, isn't she?" Eden asked me, and I ignored that too. In fact, I was doing everything in my power to ignore everything about Poppy. To build a box around her and put her away. "But." Eden took her teacup of whiskey back to her chair and sat back down. "This is where our fates intertwine." She glanced at the fireplace, cold and full of ash. "Does that thing work? It's fucking freezing in here."

"How do our fates intertwine?" Poppy asked flatly.

"Good God, you're a few steps behind." Eden sighed. "I mean, does innocence come with stupidity? I guess I'm glad I was never inflicted."

I turned away and began laying a fire to light. *Clean the ash. Place the kindling. Strike a match.*

The rote steps were a distraction from the noose tightening around all our necks.

"Fuck you," my princess snapped at Eden. "Ronan. What the hell is she getting at?"

"She is saying," I bent and breathed over the embers so they'd ignite into flame. "That the way to save your life and get the Dead or Alive order off your head is that you need to be a Morelli. And I can do that by marrying you."

I glanced over my shoulder to watch her stumble backward into the chair.

"No," she said, which I knew she'd say.

I won't be married again. For any reason.

She'd said that to me, and I'd believed her. Marriage was hell and we both knew it.

"We'll get married," I said. "And have it annulled. We won't actually be married." I stood and she was shaking her head. "We'll send Eden back with whatever proof she needs, and we'll go our separate ways."

"Ah." Eden winced. "Gonna have to stop you there. You're going to have to come back with me."

"Why?"

She sighed. "Or they'll disown me. And kill me."

"I don't give a shit," I said.

"Well, then the proof of your marriage won't be going anywhere, will it?"

Eden Morelli was a stone-cold killer. I could see it in her eyes, just like she could see it in mine. "I'll come back with you," I told her. "Poppy goes free."

"Yeah," Eden winced again. "That's not going to work either. There's that whole Dead or Alive thing. You marry her and they won't kill her, but they'll still want her alive, and that could get ugly. And," she said, smiling suddenly. "We could go another thirty rounds on who's going where, but there's the little matter of the favor Poppy owes me."

I turned to look at her as she sat down in the chair. "Favor?"

"You've got to be kidding me," she said to Eden.

"What favor?"

"My sister didn't pay her for that information I got about you," she told me.

"And," Eden said with a shrug. "She refused to sleep with me. So, she still owes me."

"That's bullshit," I said.

"What if I sleep with you now?" Poppy asked, and both Eden and I turned to look at her.

"Well, isn't that interesting?" Eden crossed her legs. "I'm intrigued, but as much as I'm willing to see past that haircut of yours, it won't do me much good. You need to get married and you both need to come back with me. It's the only way we're all getting out of this." She pulled her phone out of her pocket. "But the clock is ticking. Fuck. No service? Really?"

"Ronan?" Poppy said. "What do we do?"

"I've made it pretty clear," Eden said, and I grabbed Poppy by the elbow and pulled her outside, away from Eden.

The wind was a relentless howl.

She looked at me, and I took it for as long as I could before turning away.

"Are you all right?" she asked, concern oozing off her. It would be so easy to rest in that concern, to gather it up and let it do its job. To pretend for just a bit longer that we were still in the fantasy of the cottage. But reality was cold and hard and brutal and here.

"Fine."

She laughed at my brusque answer, but I didn't smile in return.

I reached out and touched the scratches on her neck the men had left on her. She would have a terrible bruise on her stomach too. She could have died. Again.

Another brutal truth? I'd taken shit care of her, distracted as I'd been by wanting her. By how she made me feel. I could have her or I could keep her safe, and I'd tried too hard to have both.

That's right, lad, my father's voice was back in my head. *That's the way of it.*

"We're getting married," I said.

She backed up a step, taking her comfort with her.

"There's got to be another way?" she asked. "Some window we can jump out of?" That she tried to smile tore me right in half. Enough. Enough of that fecking mess. Enough of feeling anything.

"We're out of windows."

I saw the dust first. Off the back of a car coming from town. And my blood froze. Ice filled me from head to toe and I welcomed it with open arms. I let it invade me and put me to rights.

"See that car?" I asked, turning her, grabbing her face so she was looking at the threat that was barreling toward her. "Who do you think is in that car?"

"I don't . . . I don't know."

"Right. So you can sit here and hope for the best and catch a bullet between the eyes or get snatched up by the Dubrassi Brothers who will delight in raping you six ways from Sunday before dropping you "alive" at the feet of the Morellis. Or maybe you're right and it's nothing." I feigned indifference. "But this is the feeling you'll be living with all day. Every day. So you can do the smart thing and take care of shit. Or you can do what you've done your whole goddamned life and put your head in the sand. Because it's worked out so well for you and your unborn—"

She smacked me. Hard. Which was good. Right. I'd crossed a line, but she needed to wake the fuck up.

From the boot of the car, I grabbed my bag of weapons and money.

"Come on," I said and grabbed her arm, pulling her back into the cottage. I locked the doors.

"Get down on the ground." I barked and stood with my back to the wall, looking out the side of the curtains at that car coming up the road. It came closer. And closer. Turned down the drive toward the house. I had three guns with enough bullets to fill each of them up twice.

"What have you got?" I asked Eden.

"Six bullets," she said.

Not enough. Not enough if it was the Dubrassis. They could tear this place down with firepower. *But they want Poppy alive.*

"I thought your guy was going to take care of anyone else looking for us?"

Eden actually looked scared. All she could give me was a shrug.

If I snuck out the back, circled around wide enough to get behind them. Yeah. That was what I could do. I ran to the kitchen and smashed through one of those old windows. Glass fell into the sink and out onto the stones.

Sorry, Sinead.

"It's Father Patrick," Poppy cried, having taken my place along the wall. I froze, about to climb through the jagged hole in the window. "It's just Father Patrick."

Stress was making a mess of her. I could see it. The tears in her eyes, the trembling of her lips, and I'd made so many mistakes. So many. But there was only one way to keep her safe.

"This is what it will be like," I told her. "If you don't come with us. You'll never feel safe."

She looked from me to Eden. "They'll leave my sister alone?"

"Yep."

"And they won't kill you?"

"No."

"Will they kill him?" she asked, pointing at me. *Him.* And not looking at me. *Good*, I thought. She was building her own walls. *You'll need them, princess. Where we're going, you'll need every wall you can get.*

"No. We all go back, and everyone is safe." Eden wasn't lying as much as she was hoping, and Poppy got it. There were no guarantees where we were going.

She laughed at that and when she looked at me, her eyes were dull. Resigned. "I'll be married again. And to a Morelli. Hardly seems safe."

"I'll keep you safe," I promised her.

"I don't want this," she told me. "I don't want any of this."

"Me neither."

"Perfect! A proper Morelli wedding," Eden said, standing, her eyes alight. "I don't suppose you guys know where we can find a priest?"

The three of us walked up the hill to the church. I carried a bag of money and had three guns on my body and Eden, in tall boots with tiny little heels that made no sense at all on the rocks, had another one. Poppy, in front, wore black sweatpants and a flannel shirt tied at her waist with practically no buttons. She'd resisted Eden's efforts to make her hair look "less like a nest." The cats, like they knew her, or remembered me, came out to hop along the stones.

We'd taken every knife in Sinead's kitchen and hid them on our bodies. Fully armed, Poppy was walking up the hill like she was walking to her grave. And I was following her with something like... satisfaction. I didn't have to make a choice anymore. She was mine. Under law. Under the eyes of God. I wouldn't have to wake up tomorrow and hope she was safe.

Or wonder what she was doing.

Or if she'd found that man who told her she was wonderful and fucked her in all the ways I'd refused.

The realization that I could fuck her was one I pushed away.

I could have her or I could keep her safe. Not both. Never both. So, I cultivated my anger. I considered all my plans. And the familiar cold of my life before her settled down around me, even while my heart and my brain and my body burned for her with the satisfaction of knowing—she was mine now.

To have and to hold.

✧ ✧ ✧

Poppy

THE CHURCH DOOR was heavy, and I put all my weight into pulling it open. I felt a stitch pop in my shoulder and the sting barely registered. Nothing registered. I was moving through quicksand, my brain occupied with trying to mitigate this disaster.

I remembered with a bitter, hysterical laugh how I'd mitigated the senator's cruelty. That little thing with my hand so he couldn't grind my bones together in his grip. What a tiny thing. What a silly stupid thing I was.

Survival had taken everything from me before. Pride and sense of self. Babies and a bloody painful future that I'd gotten free of. Only to be pushed into something worse.

Marriage to Ronan would grind me into dust. There was no way to protect myself. No way to hold my body or heart so they might be safe. Too late I realized never seeing him again would have been a blessing. Wanting what I couldn't have was not going to be pleasant while married to this man.

I couldn't make sense of it, and there was no talking it through with him either. He'd gone someplace deep in his head. I could see it. Someplace I couldn't follow even after everything we'd shared. He was cold and he was brutal and he was a stranger.

A Morelli, even.

Soon, he'd be my husband.

I tried to follow his lead, to let the chill of not caring fill me. I tried to look at him like he was a stranger, and with his face set in brutal terrifying lines, I could almost convince myself it was true.

"Poppy?" Father Patrick came out of the vestry with a smile and concern on his face. "Is everything all right?"

"Actually," I said with my best false smile, my implacable calm that I'd learned during all my years with the senator. "We've come to ask a favor."

"Of course." His eyes darted to Eden and then up at Ronan. Quickly, he looked back at me, his eyes wide. His smile gone. He wasn't a dumb man. He knew something was wrong. "What do you need, Poppy?"

Strangely, tears bit my eyes and I had to blink them back. Panic, maybe. Fear, for sure. And grief of the life I'd been thinking about. Beth Soeterick and her sister and school and a future—all gone. And the life I was about to go into felt like something I would not survive.

Married. To Ronan. A twisted version of my deepest desire.

"We need you to marry us, Father Patrick."

"Oh!" he exclaimed, mustering up some enthusiasm, though with one glance back at Ronan and his bleak face, it was gone. "Are you sure?"

"We are," I said, pulling his attention back to me. "And we have a time issue."

"Okay," he said. "Well, you need to register three weeks before—"

"We need to do this now," Ronan interrupted.

"Well, in Ireland, to be legal, you need the marriage notice form—"

"The form we can worry about later," Eden said.

"But—"

"You're a priest," Ronan said. "We're of age."

"I fear you're doing something that you'll regret. You'll be asking for forgiveness for this act, son—"

"I'm not your fucking son!" he shouted and then did what I was terrified he was going to do all along. He pulled a gun on the priest. "And I will not be talking about forgiveness with the likes of you."

I stepped between them and smiled with all my might. "I'm sorry, Father Patrick, to pull you into this. But we need to get married. Now."

After a long moment, Father Patrick nodded. Eden clapped. "Fabulous. I'll take pictures!"

"Follow me," Father Patrick said, leading us into the sanctuary. We then climbed the three red stairs to stand in front of the whalebone altar. Our panic and guns defiled the peace and quiet of the space. We'd brought something very unholy to a holy place.

"Use this," Ronan said and pulled from his bag the black shirt I'd worn when I'd woken up in the cottage that first morning. It was still dirty. Still stained with my blood. He tore a giant piece off it and handed it to the priest. "For the handfasting."

"That's an ancient pagan ceremony," Father Patrick said, but held the blood-stained cloth. "It hasn't been performed in the church for hundreds of years."

"Do you know it or not?" Ronan asked.

"Enough of it, I suppose."

"That's what I want," Ronan said.

"Is that what you want?" Father Patrick asked me.

"I want to be married to Ronan," I said, unclear on what handfasting was, but Ronan seemed deeply set on having it and I figured someone should get something they wanted today.

"I'll do it," Father Patrick said, and Eden breathed a sigh of relief. "On one condition."

"You're in a poor place to be demanding conditions," Ronan said.

"What is the condition?" I asked, scared he might insist Ronan forgive him. That Ronan would never do.

"Confession," Father Patrick said.

"Oh brother," Eden muttered.

"Of course," I said quickly. "I suppose I've lied and had—"

"Not yours, lass," Father Patrick pointed at Ronan. "His."

Ronan took two steps, crowding the priest against a pulpit. "Bless me, Father, for I have sinned," he said, each word bitten and sharp. "The last time I went to confession was the night Tommy hung himself. I've killed thirty-two men in my life."

I staggered back, catching myself against a baptism bowl. I mean, I knew he was a killer, but hearing it out loud made it real.

"The first when I was sixteen. Two of them just an hour ago. I imagine I'll have a few more to kill before the day is over. One of them was Poppy's fucking husband too. And I'd do it all again. I've lied. I've stolen. Though it's been years since I've had to. I've taken the Lord's name in vain every fucking day. I've had wicked thoughts. Wicked thoughts about fucking her." He pointed at me. "And just an hour ago, I had a wicked thought of watching the two of them." He pointed to Eden and me. "Fuck each other. And the last few days, I've had real wicked thoughts about killing you. And I'm not sorry for any of it."

Over Ronan's shoulder, Father Patrick met my eyes. He was shaking, he was so scared. "Are you sure, lass?" he asked me. "I see no redemption in this man. No sweetness."

I didn't either. But choice was a luxury I didn't have.

"I'm sure."

"May God have mercy on your souls," Father Patrick said. To all of us.

"Just marry us," Ronan snarled.

Father Patrick had a form in the vestry that we signed. Eden signed as a witness.

"It's not legal," he said again. "Without the stamp from the office—"

"I'll worry about the stamp," Eden said, like a doomsday wedding planner. Hysterical, I laughed and clapped a hand over my mouth.

We stood under the sunlight streaming in through the windows and the chain link fence that protected them from the boys who were long gone.

Except Ronan.

If he showed any reaction to getting married to me in the place where he'd once been terrorized and where he'd lost a friend, he didn't show it.

He will never show me anything again, I thought, and felt such grief I nearly cried.

"Take her right hand in yours," Father Patrick said, and Ronan pulled my icy fingers into his warm palm. The priest then wrapped the black shirt around our hands. "Repeat after me." He then said a long stream of things in Irish.

Ronan repeated them.

"I don't . . . I can't . . ." I stammered when it was my turn.

"It's all right, lass. Repeat after me: 'Ye are

blood of my blood.'"

"Ye are blood of my blood," I murmured to our clasped hands, unable to look at Ronan.

"Ye are bone of my bone."

"Ye are bone of my bone," I repeated. These vows were savage and so fitting for this unholy union we were making.

"Do you have any rings?" Father Patrick asked, and Ronan and I both shook our heads.

"Oh, wait!" Eden cried, coming up the three steps to stand with us beside the whalebone altar. She twisted a ring off her finger and put it in Ronan's hand. It was a dark blue stone as big as my thumbnail surrounded by a starburst of gold. It was ostentatious and not at all my style. "A Morelli heirloom," she said. "Wear it in good health." She snapped another picture on her phone and stepped back.

"Repeat after me," Father Patrick said. "With this ring, I thee wed."

"With this ring, I thee wed," Ronan said and slipped the ring on my left hand. It was a bit too big and very heavy.

"Is there a ring for Ronan?" Father Patrick asked.

"I don't need a fucking ring," Ronan muttered. "Skip it."

He wasn't mine. I knew that. This ceremony was a terrible sham, but I wore this monstrosity, marking me as his. As Morelli. He remained unchanged. Unburdened. His own person still.

"With my body, I thee worship," Father Patrick said.

"With my body, I thee worship," Ronan repeated, and my eyes flew to his, startled by the carnal words.

"You say the words as well, Poppy," Father Patrick urged.

"With my body, I thee worship," I said right to Ronan, feeling my cheeks get hot. My body taking all my adrenaline and turning it into something else.

We said other things. Promises we didn't mean. Oaths we would break the second we could.

I never thought it was possible, but this wedding felt worse than my first.

"For better or worse," Ronan repeated.

"For better or worse," I also repeated, the words throwing into terrifying relief just how bad worse could be.

"I now pronounce you man and wife," Father Patrick said. "You may kiss—"

Ronan didn't even wait for Father Patrick to

finish. He kissed me with violence. With intent. He marked me down to my blood and bone. His. Always his. Forever his.

When he stepped back, I wobbled, off-balance, caught only by our hands bound together. Which he unbound, tucking the torn cloth in his pocket. I felt precarious.

Terrified.

"Can we have a second?" I asked my husband. My voice was low and broken. "I just . . . need a second." Some kindness. Some reassurance. I needed the man who'd saved my life and scratched Rascal under the chin and made fires and held me close to show himself. For just a second.

"No time for that," Ronan said, turning to Eden. "Is this enough proof for the Morellis?"

"Get me someplace with a signal, and I'll send it all to Bryant. But he'll want to know when he can expect you in New York." Eden looked at me. "Both of you."

"I have a flight booked tomorrow morning."

Ronan grabbed his bag of guns and money and walked away. Without a second look for Father Patrick or his wife.

Twisting the ring around my finger, I thought of all the times I'd had to find the strength to face the day. The morning after my first wedding night. When Zilla burned down our house. When Dad died.

I'd done this before—pulled myself together and carried on. This, perhaps because things had happened so fast, seemed harder.

"Poppy?" Father Patrick whispered, his hand on my shoulder. "Are you all right?"

"I'm just fine," I said, and with my blinding false smile, I followed my husband.

To have and to hold.

For better and worse.

I wasn't sure how, but I knew things were going to get much worse.

✧ ✧ ✧

Thank you for reading BROKEN! We hope you loved Ronan and Poppy's emotional love story. Read the final book in UNTAMED.

Marriage has always meant violence. I don't trust it, but it's the only thing keeping me afloat in these dark undercurrents. I married for safety but I got the most dangerous thing in the world—Ronan Byrne for a husband.

Now we're returning to Bishop's Landing to face our demons. Mine. His. We have real enemies to conquer, but it's the fear in my heart that beats the loudest. I can't stop being in love with him. Except the killer with the heart of stone doesn't love me.

I don't know whose family I belong in anymore. Or whether I should stay with Ronan when this is over. But I may not live long enough to make the choice.

You can find UNTAMED on Amazon, Barnes & Noble, Apple Books, Kobo and Google Play.

And you can read the story of Winston Constantine, the oldest son in the Constantine family and head of the business empire, right now!

Money can buy anything. And anyone. As the head of the Constantine family, I'm used to people bowing to my will. Cruel, rigid, unyielding—I'm all those things. When I discover the one woman who doesn't wither under my gaze, but instead smiles right back at me, I'm intrigued.

You can find STROKE OF MIDNIGHT on Amazon, Barnes & Noble, Apple Books, Kobo and Google Play now.

The warring Morelli and Constantine families have enough bad blood to fill an ocean, and their brand new stories will be told by your favorite dangerous romance authors. See what books are available now and sign up to get notified about new releases here…

www.dangerouspress.com

About the Author

Molly O'Keefe has always known she wanted to be a writer (except when she wanted to be a florist or a chef and the brief period of time when she considered being a cowgirl). And once she got her hands on some romances, she knew exactly what she wanted to write.

She published her first Harlequin romance at age 25 and hasn't looked back. She loves exploring every character's road towards happily ever after.

Originally from a small town outside of Chicago, she went to university in St. Louis where she met and fell in love with the editor of her school newspaper. They followed each other around the world for several years and finally got married and settled down in Toronto, Ontario. They welcomed their son into their family in 2006, and their daughter in 2008. When she's not at the park or cleaning up the toy room, Molly is working hard on her next novel, trying to exercise, stalking Tina Fey on the internet and dreaming of the day she can finish a cup of coffee without interruption.

NEWSLETTER
www.molly-okeefe.com

FACEBOOK
facebook.com/MollyOKeefeBooks

INSTAGRAM
instagram.com/mokeefeauthor

About Midnight Dynasty

Midnight Dynasty is a brand new world where enemies and lovers are often one and the same.

JOIN THE FACEBOOK GROUP HERE
www.dangerouspress.com/facebook

FOLLOW US ON INSTAGRAM
www.instagram.com/dangerouspress

SIGN UP FOR THE NEWSLETTER
www.dangerouspress.com

Copyright

This is a work of fiction. Any resemblance to actual persons, living or dead, business establishments, events or locales is entirely coincidental. All rights reserved. Except for use in a review, the reproduction or use of this work in any part is forbidden without the express written permission of the author.

Broken © 2021 by M. O'Keefe
Print Edition

Cover design by Book Beautiful

Printed in Great Britain
by Amazon